Pra

A J Dalt

'Unique ideas and a story that develops in an unpredictable manner.' - Fantasy-Faction.com

'Gives you an interesting setting and a devilishly good villain.' - SFX

'Engaging, filled with sacrifice, adventure and some very bloody battles!' - SciFi Now magazine

"Divine, divisive and downright dastardly!"
– Carl Rhinebeck

"Contains secrets, magicks, feisty familiars, warnings and true beauty. A must-read!"
-Kate Sultrow on The Book of Witches

'There's interesting world building to discover and a surprising amount of dry humour to enjoy. A great deal of fun and certainly worthy of your time!'- The Eloquent Page

‘With its rich tapestry of characters and incident there is never a dull moment.’
- FantasyBookReview.co.uk

‘The best young British fantasy author on the circuit at the moment.’ - Waterstones central buyer

‘Very, very clever and manages to offer something different over the traditional fantasy fare. Different, fresh and unique.’ - Sfbook.com

‘A. J. Dalton’s world building is fresh with new ideas.’ - IWillReadBooks.com

‘Fast moving and keeps you gripped at all times, while also creating a world with immense depth and complexity. Five stars!’- Amazon Review

‘A J Dalton, thank you, what I’ve read will stay with me for a long time.’- *GoodReads.com*:

‘Dalton’s characters are complex and he has ways of twisting events and viewpoints that will often surprise me (in a good way!)! Politics, mythology and magic are woven into the fabric of the story creating a rich tapestry.’ - Amazon Review

The Book of Demons

A J Dalton

kristell-ink.com

ISBN 978-1-913562-23-6 (Hardback)
ISBN 978-1-913562-24-3 (Paperback)
ISBN 978-1-913562-25-0 (EPUB)

Cover art by Charlotte Pang
Typesetting by Book Polishers

Kristell Ink
An Imprint of Grimbold Books
5 St John's Way,
Hempton,
Oxfordshire,
OX15 0QR
United Kingdom

www.kristell-ink.com

Dedicated to every woman, person or animal who has suffered persecution or demonization for who they are.

Contents

An Introduction: Demons among Us

As reported in London's *Catholic Herald* in 2019, in recent years there has been a possibly surprising but dramatic surge in the number of exorcisms being performed by the Catholic Church throughout the world, including in the US. The *Catholic Herald* based its story on a researched academic article that was produced by Dr R.A. Chesnut of Virginia Commonwealth University and Dr K. Kingsbury of the University of Alberta: 'Driving out the devil: what's behind the exorcism boom?', 2019. Indeed, Pope Francis himself has personally conducted an exorcism, and in 2018 convened an exorcism workshop in the Vatican that was attended by 250 priests from 51 countries.

One might wonder what is behind such a surge. Could it be as simple as the Catholic Church *promoting* its faith via the practice of exorcisms and a belief in the manifestation of demons in the real world? Actually, it cannot be as simple as that since it would appear the Catholic Church has only acted based on a prior extremely significant increase in the general public's conviction that demons exist, that demonic possession is all too real and that more exorcisms are therefore required. Indeed, polls run by both Gallup and the data firm YouGov over a number of decades indicate an increasing number of Americans (up to 50%) believe in demonic possession. The percentage who believe in the devil is even higher, and has been growing: Gallup polls show that the number rose from 55% in 1990, to 70% in 2007.

No matter your perspective (religious or non-religious), the above is surely alarming. Either Satan's actual influence upon our world is increasingly manifest and widespread, or the general public is increasingly susceptible to religious messaging, the sorts of suggestions delivered via social media and entertainment channels, socio-religious hysteria and/or a rejection of science-based Rationalism in this 'post-truth' era. Although the latter understanding of what is going on might be supported by citing specific examples such as the mass-reporting and mass-hysteria concerning vampires in Malawi in 2017…

"Dozens of Malawians claim they are being attacked by 'vampires'. Victims say 'vampires' break into their homes and drink their blood. [It all] feeds rumours about innocent people in areas where belief in vampires is strong. Tales of 'vampires' has seen several revenge mob attacks on suspects" (*The Daily Mail*, UK)

… at the same time, the UK's 'post-Christian' general public might/should be far less susceptible when it comes to such messaging, suggestion and hysteria than in times past. After all, in 2016, the Church of England reported that the national congregation had fallen below one million for the first time (and the congregation was down to 750,000 by 2019), and in the same year NatCen's British Social Attitudes survey reported that 'The number of people who say they have no religion is escalating and significantly outweighs the Christian population in England and Wales.'

That leaves us with something of a paradox: the UK is potentially more cynical than ever about the existence of demons, and yet exorcism is 'now an industry' in the UK, the latter identified by a government-ordered inquiry in 2020 and reported by *The Telegraph* newspaper. One explanation (among several) that might occur to us is that demons are not actually a matter of faith or belief at all – rather, they might instead be a matter of fact or reality.

If we (whether religious or otherwise) were to start considering demons as a matter of fact or reality, that could cause us to start wondering about their specific and concrete nature, characteristics and origins. Such a deliberation is known as *demonology*, that pseudo-scientific search for, examination of and experimentation with regard to the truly demonic. We might do well to pause before delving further into demonology or embarking upon any pursuit of the demonic, since such delving and pursuit might only bring us closer to demonkind, into a dangerous proximity or into a sphere of unhealthy influence and temptation. As the great philosopher of the Middle Ages Albertus Magnus (1200-1280) put it, and he was known as *Doctor Universalis* and *Doctor Expertus*, eventually becoming a Catholic saint:

> "It is taught by the demons, it teaches about the demons, and it leads to the demons."

***

Demonisation within the Bible

Tentative as we might now be concerning our investigation into both demons and demonology, if we start with the Bible as a main source of information then, surely, we will be on fairly safe ground. After all, the Bible is often considered a book of holy spells with which one of the faithful might exorcise all demons, Satan included, as per the influential movie *The Exorcist* (1973).

The Bible is unambiguous concerning the ability of demons to possess both humans and animals in the real world, thereby to lead or tempt individuals away from God and towards sin (Matthew 8: 28-33), yet also to influence the affairs of humankind more broadly. In the Book of Revelation, the ancient Greek city of Pergamon (now in modern eastern Turkey) was 'where Satan live[d]' and had his throne. It was a city that both worshipped a multiplicity of older Greco-Roman and Egyptian gods and also provided the site of one of Christianity's seven major churches in Asia Minor. However, come 92CE, the city's Christian priest named Antipas was roasted to death in the Brazen Bull by pagan priests for refusing to declare the Roman emperor as 'lord and god' above all. It is thus that Jesus instructs John of Patmos:

> "To the angel of the church in Pergamon write:
> These are the words of him who has the sharp, double-edged sword. I know where you live – where Satan has his throne. Yet you remain true to my name. You did not renounce your faith in me, not even in the days of Antipas, my faithful witness, who was put to death in your city – where Satan lives."
>
> (Revelation 2: 12-13)

With Pergamon 'demonised' as the home of Satan, its temples described as Satan's throne, and the murderous attack on the priest of Christianity representing the action by which the devil 'lives', Satan becomes the personification of all pagan or non-Christian religions and all physical and political attacks upon Christianity. He is synonymous with bloody sacrifice, scheming, false idols, lies, cunning tests, death and brutality, fire and screaming, the animalistic, and a struggle for dominance and dominion. It is not surprising, therefore, that his physical representation and description in the Bible is marked by the animals most commonly deified by the Greco-Roman and Egyptian temples of Pergamon: the horned bull and the winged serpent. The New Testament (NT) claims that the serpent in the Old Testament's Garden of Eden is one of Satan's avatars, and then he is variously described as 'an enormous red dragon with seven heads and ten horns and seven crowns', 'a dragon that can spew water like a river', 'the beast', one who can mark the heads and hands of his followers (666) and 'a thorn in the flesh'.

Pergamon is also a vision of what Satan wants for all of humankind and all of the earth: it is his political ambition, ideology and violent desire. He seeks to prevent God's creation being a heaven-on-earth, by establishing his own throne on earth (in Pergamon) and overseeing some hell or dark underworld (as per the temple of Serapis in Pergamon, the god having an Osiris/Hades aspect with Anubis/Cerebus sitting at his feet) that is a place of horror, roasting flame (the Brazen Bull), torture, unholy spectacle and the public witnessing, endorsement or celebration of both sinful and sacrilegious acts. It is the exact opposite of the Kingdom of Heaven: it is literally hell-on-earth. It is not a place of 'light' (for Jesus is 'the light of the world', in John 8); rather, it is a place of darkness and the fires of punishment.

From the above, we can begin to understand the 'demonisation' of Satan and his acts as both a metaphorical personification and actual description of the physical and political persecution that Christians were suffering during the extended period of the NT's writing. Just as the nature of that persecution of and the opposition to Christianity changes with time, so the qualities of Satan shift and expand so that all anti-Christian acts may be included. Ultimately, Satan must come to be the antagonist (the Dark Lord) set against everything that Christianity represents, and must perform the attempt to bring down heaven itself to replace God the King in some sort of military coup. Thus, the dramatic climax or the 'story' of the war in heaven at the end of the Bible (Revelation), when Satan attempts a coup, is logically inevitable.

> Then war broke out in heaven, Michael and his angels
> fought against the dragon, and the dragon and his angels

> fought back. But he was not strong enough, and they lost their place in heaven. The great dragon was hurled down – that ancient serpent called the devil, or Satan, who leads the whole world astray. He was hurled to the earth and his angels with him.
>
> (Revelation 12)

It is with the quote above that the true nature of demons proper is revealed: they are those angels who followed Satan in his war against heaven, thus becoming 'fallen angels'. With their potential for an angelic appearance, we can then apprehend how demons, in their corruption, might be able to seduce or tempt us with their looks and promise of sexual infidelity, to draw us towards them and away from the holy sacrament of marriage, to have us follow them as they in turn follow Satan. It is precisely such a set of messages that can be read when the Book of Revelation presents us with the Whore of Babylon: 'Babylon the Great, the Mother of Harlots and Abominations of the Earth'. The Whore is explicitly described as sitting upon the self-same 'scarlet coloured beast [...] having seven heads and ten horns' (Revelation 17: 3) as Satan is elsewhere described. She is undoubtedly attractive, for 'when I saw her, I wondered with great admiration' (17: 6), yet of course the danger she represents is not just to the narrator, for she has also fornicated with and politically compromised 'the kings of the earth [...] and the inhabitants of the earth' (17: 2) in order to 'reign[...] over' (17: 18) them. Therefore, we see that the Whore works as a follower of Satan, in service to his throne on earth and his global ideopolitical ambitions.

Much of the demonic nature is revealed to us by the Bible, seemingly. At the same time, we cannot ignore the partial and propagandist tendency the Bible has in (mis)appropriating the features of the Greco-Roman and Egyptian gods and (re) assigning them as features of Satan and his followers i.e. literally *demonising* them. (Even the term demon represents something of a misappropriation, since it comes from the ancient Greek – δαίμων *daimōn* – but has the original meaning of 'a divine spirit of inspiration'.) Yes, it is perhaps just fighting back against the terrible persecution suffered by Antipas and many other Christians – even as a matter of self-defence or basic survival – yet its overtly satirical and symbolic (not to mention visionary) nature must bring into question just how real or actual demons are.

Whether it was because later thinkers, theologians and demonologists recognised the political recasting of other faiths and cultures in the Bible or whether it was because they appreciated that all writers (including the various authors of the Bible) implicitly draw upon their socio-historic context, culture, education and personal life experiences, they were in accord that an increased understanding of and insight into the Bible could be achieved via a study and consideration of the cultures and texts which preceded or were contemporaneous with the Bible, perhaps then to derive new or further revelations from or via the Bible. Hence, investigations into demonkind and demonic nature moved beyond the limitations of the Bible's text, to more ancient or equally ancient texts, such as the Book of Enoch (300-100BCE), which contained 'unique' information concerning demons and giants (the Nephilim) and would have been known by Jews and early Near Eastern Christians.

***

The Great Demonologists

We might wonder for what the demonologists of various eras were searching specifically. It seems that many were intent upon finding a way to combat the threat represented to humankind by Satan and his demons – to find the means of our very salvation. Once accessed, that hidden knowledge would facilitate the Second Coming of Christ, as precisely described in the Book of Revelation when John of Patmos (the same John that Jesus spoke to about Pergamon being where Satan lived) has an apocalyptic vision concerning a scroll secured by the Seven Seals of God – with the opening of each seal, a different manner of demon will be released as a terror upon the earth, until all the seals are undone and the end of days occurs. At the same time, once all the seals are undone, the knowledge within the scroll will be accessed, revealing how to bring about the Second Coming... should the one opening the scroll be inclined to bring about such salvation, of course. Hence, identifying the seals which could bind, summon and control demonkind became the obsession of demonologists through the ages, who – through their research and learning – thought to discover the powers of the dark magician, the necromancer and the unholy conjuror.

These demonologists researched and gathered texts and fragments from the ancient civilizations and compiled their findings in books of their own, books that became known as grimoires, for the knowledge they contained made them spell-books – or books of black magic – which enabled the command of demons. One of the most famous works is *The Grand Grimoire*, also known as *Le Dragon Rouge* or *The Red Dragon* (a direct reference to Satan's description in the Book of Revelation), which gives instructions for summoning Lucifer himself, for the purpose of then doing a 'deal with the devil'. The earliest date cited for the grimoire is 1421, but most critics believe it was compiled by Antonio Venitiana del Rabina in the c.19. Be that as it may, apart from sections apparently based on some of King Solomon's own writings, much of the contents derive from *The Key of Solomon* (c.14 or 15) and *The Lesser Key of Solomon* (c.17), the latter anonymously authored but derived from writings of the c.16. These grimoires, along with their instructions, provide drawings of the various seals, sigils and pentagrams (synonymous with non- and pre-Christian faiths) which can be used for summoning and binding demons of particular 'rank' and name, such classifications usually based either upon the ranks of European nobility or the seven deadly sins (described with such power in the c.13-14 works of Dante, but originating from a c.4 Greco-Roman tradition). Another well-known set of grimoires (c.17 onwards) exists under the collective title of *The Book of Saint Cyprian*, claiming to be based on the work of the c.3 Saint Cyprian of Antioch (now in modern Turkey, like Pergamon), a pagan sorcerer who converted to Christianity.

What the reader may notice from the above is that a majority of the grimoires emerged in Europe during the c.15-17, but that they based themselves either on multiple NT-era, late medieval or early Renaissance texts. There is a process and tradition here of looking to pass on religious or arcane knowledge that might otherwise be lost, a tradition which may well have started with the destruction of the Second Temple in Jerusalem in 70CE, and the realisation among Jewish scholars that, with the loss of their central place of gathering and sharing, the oral tradition of passing on knowledge was no longer sustainable: instead, such teaching and thought needed to be developed and written down over the ensuing decades and centuries, providing us with (amongst other texts) the Talmud of the Jewish faith.

As just one example of how this process or tradition has continued to feed non Biblical secrets, ideas and attitudes through to our current understanding of the demonic, we might consider the character of Lilith, Adam's first wife in the Garden of Eden according to the Babylonian Talmud, *although Lilith is not even mentioned in the Bible.* The legend of Lilith developed significantly during the Middle Ages, before becoming a fully-fledged narrative within the Zohar, a foundational work of Jewish mystical thought which first appeared in c.13 Spain, published by the Jewish writer Moses de Leon: refusing to be ruled over by Adam, Lilith leaves the Garden of Eden to mate with the archangel Samael (read as

Satan) and be transformed into a succubus and the Queen of Demons; then becoming jealous of Adam and his new wife, Lilith looks to steal away their children during the night, to ruin their happiness, to lead them into despair, to have them forsake God, and to lead them to Satan thereby. Here, then, we have the patriarchal version of Christianity demonising the female once more (as with the Whore of Babylon and even Eve in the Bible) as sexually corrupt and corrupting, an agent of Satan and a witch or night-hag.

The narrative concerning the malign female witch who consorts with demonic familiars was to be used all too frequently during the Spanish Inquisition, of course, and during the reigns of Henry VIII (who introduced the first Witchcraft Act), Elizabeth I (who oversaw the political purging of Catholics from England and Scotland), and James I (who similarly looked to persecute Catholic 'enemies' under the auspices of his book *Daemonologie*, written and published in 1599). The British throne literally demonised its political opponents and then visited suffering and slaughter them. It was a time of witch hunts, terrible torture, public execution, false accusation and religious persecution – just as Antipas had once suffered in Pergamon – and once again a demonic and demonising narrative was to serve as a form of self-justifying political propaganda, a propaganda that was only strengthened and popularised by Christopher Marlowe's play *Doctor Faustus* (1588-93) and Shakespeare's *Macbeth* (1606).

All that said, the demonic narrative of that time was not entirely propagandist, for Elizabeth I had the notorious dark magician, astrologer, alchemist, mathematician and Hermetic philosopher Doctor John Dee (1527-1609) as both a member of her court and a political adviser: Marlowe's Doctor Faustus was based on an actual demonologist, therefore. Dee was an extremely learned and well-travelled man who gave notable university lectures around Europe, and who would not have thought of all the disciplines he had mastered as 'separate' subjects (as we would nowadays). He owned a mirror of obsidian via which the spirits of the dead could be viewed and consulted, and it is an object which can still be seen in the British Museum, London. However, his principal area of study was in summoning angels and seeking to understand their divine language, a language that he believed underpinned nature and God's Creation, since 'In the beginning there was the Word, and the Word was God'. He continued with his research full-time when he retired from court, becoming the warden of Chetham's religious college in Manchester (now the School of Music) in 1595, at the venerable age of 68. Unfortunately, though, what with demons also being understood as angels (albeit 'fallen'), the local population accused him of summoning and consorting with devils, fiends who terrorised the city and caused various outbreaks of plague and disease. Ultimately, a mob marched on Chetham's and set fire to the 'Satanist's' library, destroying much of Dee's work. In 1605, he left Manchester weary of the struggle and returned home to Mortlake in London, where he saw out his remaining days. John Dee's library had been one of the greatest of his day, but only five of his books survived the fire at Chetham's, the margins of those books full of Dee's notes and drawings. It is said he successfully deciphered the language by which he could communicate with angels… and demons.

Yet others were to take some of Dee's Hermetic philosophy forward, up to the current day. One of the most famous occultists to do so was Aleister Crowley (1875-1947), who integrated Eastern practices with Western magical practices from the Hermetic Order of the Golden Dawn, and helped evolve the Hermetic religion known as Thelema, the name derived from the classical Greek term for our divine 'will'. Crowley's Thelema was based on *The Book of Law*, which was dictated during a spiritual experience (Egypt, 1904) by the divine being Aiwass (an avatar of the Egyptian god Horus) speaking through Crowley's wife, Rose, a god whom the Book of Revelation would of course have considered demonic. *The Book of Law* laid out the precepts of the faith (which included '"Do what thou wilt" shall be the whole law', 'Love is the law, love under will' and 'Every man and every woman is a star'), but Crowley was a prolific scholar and writer, going on to write *The Holy Books of Thelema*. Although Crowley was widely denounced in the British press for his drug-fuelled and sexually promiscuous lifestyle, ultimately seeing him evicted by the Italian government in 1923 from the religious commune he had established in Sicily, his legacy lives on. Not only does Thelema survive, with Crowley celebrated as one of its prophets, but both the religion and Crowley's thinking in general inspired the development of Wicca, feeding into the wider rise of Modern Paganism, as well as the practice of 'chaos magick' and certain forms of Satanism.

Perhaps, then, the *Doctor Universalis*, Albertus Magnus, was right when he warned us about the pursuit of demonology so long ago:

> "*It is taught by the demons, it teaches about the demons, and it leads to the demons.*"

***

A very Modern Demon

Where does that leave us? Well, it leaves us with a UK where record numbers of exorcisms are being performed, and where Wicca is recognised and supported by the local council in cities such as Milton Keynes, and a US where there is as great a conviction as ever that demons are a reality, and where The Satanic Temple group is very politically active. It leaves us with a language and culture in which we freely speak of someone having the devil in them, or fighting our 'inner demons', or a child being a 'cheeky devil', or footballers playing like 'a person possessed'. Many a person still demands that we say 'Bless you!' so that they cannot be demonically possessed again after they have sneezed the devil out of themselves.

One might have expected scientific development and new technologies to see a general decline in religious belief around the world, but it actually seems to be belief in science that is under threat these days. Yes, the Church of England has seen drastic falls in congregations, but the US and Africa are sending increasing numbers of missionaries to the UK, and multiculturalism has seen increasing populations of other faiths. And is it a coincidence that every major religion recognises demons? Maybe not. It seems, then, the demon is here to stay, whether we like it or not.

The tales contained in this book will hopefully serve either to entertain or at least provide you with salutary warning. Whether you take them seriously or not, we do so hope that you find them fiendishly enjoyable and devilishly diverting. (Amen.)

Dr Adam Dalton-West, Doctor Diabolicus, December 2020
Ravenscourt Park, London, UK

Divine Right

By Nadine Dalton-West

London, England - 1607

In the aftermath of the play, the air is thick and tight with the smell of grease, wax, warm human bodies. The room in Whitehall is a small one. Properties and costumes litter the floor, and candles gutter in sconces. The master of the candles knows, down to the minute, how long to trim his wicks to last out Mr Shakespeare's latest. The villain, the wench and the King are all dead, and out go the candles, pop, pop, one by one. It is, some say, a kind of witchcraft, but they glance behind them before they do, and they do not say it loudly in the current company.

The King – the living one, the Scottish one, not the dead one returned magically to life as a sweating player with his eyeliner running down his cheek – has left off applauding and nodding. His eyes glitter queerly. He gathers himself. He is leaving.

It is an awkward progress. The King has an odd gait, a stamping leg and a trailing one, to accompany his strange eyes and habit of lolling his tongue over his lower lip. His men bustle after him as he departs, holding doors, lifting the corners of robes, murmuring all the while. They follow by rank, his men. It shifts and changes, and members of the court can divine whose arse to kiss and who to shun at table according to which beard twitches closest to the ears of Old Jim. Today, it is Villiers. Tomorrow, who knows? The last man to exit, far from the King's bosom, scrabbling to keep up, trips over his own feet as he lets the tapestry curtain fall.

Behind him, the chamberlains and members of the King's Men fall to work. They have windows to open, the floor to sweep clean of nut shells, dog shit, spilled beer. Onstage, actors strip and douse themselves in water from wooden buckets. "At least this one doesn't hang about," says the young man still half-wearing a white dress. "The Old Queen, God rest her soul, do you recall, Dick?"

"Do I? Took her an hour to leave a room. Reckon the King likes his fawning done in private."

The young man rubs greasy lye soap between his hands. He draws breath, thinks twice, soaps his body in the silence. He tries again. "Is Master Shakespeare pressing his good fortune here?"

The elder, Dick Burbage, raises one eyebrow. "If he was running risks, we'd be the ones standing between him and a sword-point. As usual. I cannot say, Ned. The King seems well pleased."

"Demons dancing on a cliff, though? With a thousand noses? Poor Tom possessed? That's not piss-taking, think you?"

Dick sighs. "I've not read His Majesty's book. Has Will? Wager on it. You played The Scottish Play last winter, Ned. Will said the new King would be flattered. Everything the boys chucked into the cauldron and every *double double* meant something, be sure on that."

"And we're not hanged yet."

A silence. Ned soaps his hair. Dick folds a petticoat, slowly. "Not yet."

A door opens, and the two fall silent. "What ails you?" asks the man who enters. "I've seen a pair of whores swapping pox remedies look less furtive. Buck up. Did you like my raw eggs,

Ned? Chap down the front looked fit to vomit. Out, vile jelly!" He fills the room with a rolling laughter that booms back from every corner, every beam. John Hemming is possible to ignore, but only through concerted effort.

Ned has finished washing himself. He towels down, pulls on breeches and a white smock shirt, and sits himself on a low stool to pull on his boots. "'Twas fair work, Jack. It tickles them, to see a good blinding."

John draws breath, and Ned can feel a story coming, and girds himself against the onslaught of a Hemming anecdote complete with swords, double-dealing, wenches and a comically-placed cat, but before John can utter a sound the air shifts, and a shadow falls, and there is the sudden presence of a man next to them both. Ned turns.

Silently, on velvet feet, George Villiers has come back into the room. He is close. He smiles slightly, bearing sharp little teeth.

"Sire," Ned mumbles. John, the wind taken from his sails, coughs apologetically. He bows the tight bow of a man unused to deference.

"Gentlemen," says Villiers. He lifts his left hand, makes clear the large white pearl he holds between thumb and forefinger. "His Majesty wishes to send a message to Master Shakespeare. May I request an audience?"

Ned looks around. He nods at one of the boys, and the boy trots off obediently to the rear of the house, ducking through a heavy curtain, his shouts for Will immediately muffled as it falls again. "He shall be with you directly, God willing," Ned says.

"Delightful," says the man. Ned can get a good look at him now: he has high, arched brows, a long nose, a touch of felinity to cheeks and eyes. His beard is kempt, and his lips are a vivid pink between the darkness of beard and moustaches. Those lips part, suddenly. "I enjoyed your play," says Villiers. "The Bastard, in particular, pleased me." Ned nods. The role is a fine one, one of Master Shakespeare's best; it is savage and cruel, and sensuous, and doomed.

"I thank you, sir," says Ned.

New steps, now. Quick, efficient. Will Shakespeare strides, these days. "My Lord," he says, and folds into a deep, fluid bow. No reluctance. Will Shakespeare has made deference into art, and thence into gold. "You honour us."

"His Majesty honours you, sir," Villiers replies.

"His Majesty was pleased, then?"

"Oh quite so. His Majesty King James would have it be known to you, via his humble messenger here, that you see into his very soul and out again through his very eyes, and his Majesty's heart is warmed by your understanding." Ned snorts, as he cannot help but imagine Will Shakespeare turned to vapour and seething through the King's body, eyes, soul, heart and all; he is rewarded with a dark look indeed.

Villiers extends his long, thin fingers, and the pearl is magnificent in the gloom. "From His Majesty," he says. "With these words for you, Master Shakespeare: he loves you because you understand, and because you know what he knows."

Will Shakespeare takes the hand, cups it, almost caresses it, and Ned gazes at him, and in his eyes there is something awfully gentle, like pity.

Villiers's eyes blink, and something in them glitters.

***

Lothian, Scotland - 1590

The cliffs could make a good man giddy. There is something about the continual rush and hiss of the waves; even when a man is standing steady, his eyes and ears are uneasy. This is where it happened, insists His Majesty, and Alderman Kane is not so foolhardy as to argue. If King James says that the women of Berwick stood here, in this place, to summon spirits, conjure the whirlwind, to drown the steeples and, moreover, to drown the King and his new bride as they sailed back from Rotterdam, then the King must be believed.

Does Alderman Kane believe that Libby Good, Bess Skirving, Esme Jenks, are witches? Alderman Kane holds two thoughts at once. First, that simple Bess Skirving could not raise a loaf of bread in a good oven for want of trying, or her own husband's cock in his breeches, let alone a devil dancing reels over the Hook of Holland.

Second, this…

Demons must walk, if the King says they do. Witches must conjure. And the King himself comes here tonight, and Alderman Kane must find him his witches.

(He holds his copy of the King's book close, runs his thumbs over the stitching. *Daemonologie*. A little gilt, but not too much: we are not papists, after all, and Kane would despise luxury, were he to handle it.)

The waves do hiss, though.

Alderman Kane walks back to town, briskly.

***

The jailer is comically well-suited to the role. Thick-bodied, with a rolling gait, he looks like a man one would avoid after dark; he looks like a man familiar with both sides of pain. His keys bark and shrill in the lock that opens the iron door. Kane goes through, and his soft leather soles whisper on the stone floor. It is not cold stone: the jail is below ground, and the stone is close to warm, like the flanks of something living. The corridor is long. There is one window, deep-set into the wall, which does little to lighten or cleanse the air.

The cell where the women wait is pungent. It has been made clear that the King will want to see thorough work done, and so the jailer has been meticulous. Three heads, dusted with stubble, rotten eggs in a filthy nest. Alderman Kane can see from here that their hands are broken: nails gone, fingers not quite where fingers should be, but at angles and sharps. Bess Skirving slumps as though her bones have quite gone, a quietly panting mass, face obscured. Libby Good croons to herself, quite gone from this place, rocking very gently from side to side. Esme Jenks, though, looks up at him with a cat's ferocity through narrowed eyes.

"Come by to watch, sir?" There is no deference in the "sir". It is a hiss.

"Be silent," he says.

"You missed the show. The breaking. The whipping. Maybe a man of fine tastes like yours would have liked the shaving. They had a priest do that part. He would hate to have missed the mark of the devil, sir." She reaches across to Libby Good. Her broken hands cannot grip: she pushes the catatonic girl's skirt upwards with the back of her misshapen claw. He notices then the dark wine-stain covering her lap, and before he can fully avert his eyes, he sees that it is not only these women's heads that have been scalped, not only their heads that have thin blackening cuts where the work has been rough.

Kane refuses to shudder. "Stop that," he commands. "Have some godly shame in you yet, woman." He thinks Esme Jenks coughs, but the low growl coalesces into guttural laughter that shakes her thin shoulders. He looks around for the jailer, but the man has not followed behind Kane. Perhaps he can no longer bear the stink and the sound.

She tracks his glance. "Looking for Lennox? He's a piece of God's own work, is he not?" She tries to stand, but cannot. "My Pa could do with a butcher like him at killing time. Perhaps he ought to come calling."

Something in the grovelling, guttural woman provokes his bile: Kane has pity, yes, but mixed with disgust. "Your pa's a farmer?" he asks.

"Fields, stables or church," she says. "Sowing and slaughtering. Same story in the almanac as the testaments."

This is heresy. Kane sucks air through his teeth. "God in his mercy does not slaughter..." he begins. He stops. For some reason he finds it hard to speak his thought.

"Smiting? Sodom and Gomorrah? Sacrificing? Drowning?"

"You know your scripture. You can read?"

Her gaze is pitying. "As well as you, sir. Better, perhaps. Since if you see mercy, maybe you don't read what I read. God drowned all of creation. Has your good King Jacob never thought it was his own precious God longing to plunge him into the North Sea? Back in old habits, as they say."

Kane suppresses his grimace. Catlike, the thought comes again, but this wench has the arrogance of the animal too. To one side of her, Bess Skirving begins to cough. Slowly, very slowly, she rises, lifts her bruised face, spits a mixture of spittle and blood. Rabbit in the snare, he thinks. The red froth.

Animals. The sense of animals. The force holding in his words. The reading and the heresy and the... of a sudden, Alderman Kane is mortally afraid. He has studied, and he is no mean theologian. In rooms filled with men, with their noise and smell and breath and size, he has debated scripture and the law.

In this room full of women, now he shudders. He is seized with the cold certainty that he is surrounded by witches.

He takes his whip from his belt. Alderman Kane is a rational, learned man. Rationally, learnedly, he unfurls it. The woman rears back. Bess stares dumbly, the devil's mess coating her chin. He draws up his arm. The crack of the whip as it comes down is shocking.

"Now I do see you," he says. "Devil. I call you Satan, who is come into these women, dealt with by these women. Back," he says, "back," and is not sure as he is saying it whether he is exhorting something back to hell or urging Esme back from him. He strikes with the whip again, and they flinch but do not move, the three, and oh dear God, the crone and the dumb mother and the maiden, though she is surely no maiden now she is the devil's bitch? "Did you conjure?" he cries. "Were you atop the cliff, meeting, conspiring, dealing with demons?"

She comes close again. He can smell her breath, rank and meaty. "Not just I, sir. Oh, what a hag's army we had, dancing on the cliffs. Drinking whisky and singing and riding one another like the devil was in us, burning hot fires and drinking to the death of men like you."

She draws herself up. Stretches out one hideous hand, and her shaved head and high cheekbones are in strange shadow, and Kane feels something like terror loosen his knees, his bowels.

He cries out as he strikes her down. His whip splits her cheek open. She screams, and the others open their jaws like snakes and scream, and he runs.

***

The King comes here tonight, goes the buzz, the buzz of east coast voices, not burred like highland Scots and not pinched and throat-strangled like the English, but excitable, broad, song-like. King James, King James, shushing and hissing like waves against the cliffs. The sixth, the sixth, the sixth.

Alderman Kane would have scoffed internally this morning. He would have thought the susurrus around the town square evidence of sweet dedication and little thinking.

But on this day he has fought with a succubus, and gazed Lucifer in the eyes.

In his hand he clutches the good King's book, and fingers the soft ends of its pages over and over again, and when the carriage bursts around the corner in a symphony of metal on stone with the hot stink of horses, Alderman Kane falls to his knees and weeps tears of joy, and whispers, "God save the

King."

***

Bergen Harbour, Norway - 1589

From the personal log of Captain O'Connor

Such fair and foul weather have I not seen, as when we put out to sea the sight was a bonny one such as might befit a painting. It is hard to convey in words the prettiness of the quayside in the port of Rotterdam, as crowds flocked in waving hats and pretty linens to greet the royal couple: handsome they both were, beyond doubt, she in her travelling dress of green velvet and he in leather breeches and the finest lace of all Holland at cuff, at throat and upon his sleeves too, a very dovecote of frills and feathers upon King James, both waving at faces so kindly too. And all did smile upon them, new wed and young and she with a fine high brow, he not fair of face but well made in his body and with kindness in his eyes.

So aboard they came, both, neither minding of the little ceremonies we undertake, for we are superstitious folk who plough the waves, and King and princess both minded not to take the salt and bread and to tip over a glass of sack for the waters, and the princess laughed most prettily and in her high, lisping voice said that the cabins were "sharming". At dinner they were both gay in spirits, and the King said say a prayer (naturally in the New Faith, and in English, which we did not mind for his sincerity was written on his face and on his fingers, steepled as tenderly as any maiden's as he entreated Almighty God.)

Thus I cannot tell a lie, I believed us sound set for Fife, and the wind caught fair in our sails and we were underway.

At around nightfall, though, began the first of two strange

matters. The first, as crew and guests began their nightly ablutions, came a small tempest, the which was not from sky nor ocean, but from our princess. First within the cabin that was hers alone, our finest, my second mate made report on sobbing and voices raised; this distressed him, because it augurs not well aboard ship for there to be women at all, and discord in them is most serious. On investigation, she was surely weeping. I knocked. There came a banging within, a sharp word, and then Her Royal Highness threw open the door and past me she came, face red and swollen, so close as to even touch my sleeve and hand as she marched out and towards the stairs leading above decks.

Behind her, full clothed, kneeling: the King. His eyes were closed, he rocked a little, back and forth. He prayed. On his own cheeks, the evidence of tears. Not my place, that, I bethought me. I reached one bend forward and closed the door. Sending a man above to secure the princess, I drank myself a draught of good whisky and put in for bed.

I need tell little of what happened then, later into the deep stillness of night: how, out of sight of land on both sides, the air and the waves both started up and grew themselves into terrible columns, and the vessel smashed between them. First one way, then the next, we lurched like a drunkard or a madman. Sometimes we would top a wave and teeter horribly, the anticipation seething in our bellies, before the plunge that came later than a man might think possible and seemed endless, as though the fall would take us down into the very maw of hell itself, before smashing hull on wave once more.

Men flew into the air like dolls. "Lash up," I told those as could hear me, and those within sight began to strap themselves to beams and posts, wrapping the leather tawses snug around their arms or waists. A high keening grew, a mewling sound more horrible coming from the lips of seasoned sailors, forcing its way into the air and spreading like poison, and the poison went into our minds and our hearts, and I would swear that not a man aboard believed he would see morning, not then, with the world dissolved into foam and falling.

Hours passed. Numbed, past hope, we barely recognised when day broke and the seas quieted. But there was light through the round scuttles, and there was calm, and we could hear again.

The little princess and the King were both safe in their cabin. When I pushed open the door to check on them, both were grey-green and shaking, the night-pan full and the sheets vilely soiled, and the princess was still weeping; this time, unlike last night, her face was not filled with rage, but bewilderment. She reminded me in that moment, God forgive me, of a mare whipped beyond endurance.

The King left his bed, tucked her safely inside the blankets and patted his hand once, twice, on her side. Crossing the room he bared his arm to show me a bruise, livid and deep purple. When I asked if he had tumbled in the night, in the awful storm, he shook his head and curled back his queer, greenish lips. "That was no natural storm," he said.

"Sire," I began, and then stopped, for I could not contradict His Majesty. "What think you else, then?"

"Devils," he answered. "Witches. Satan's brides summoning demonic forces. They cannot bear that I come to shore with my dear bride, and so they raise the storm against God's anointed servant."

"Indeed?"

"The devil's mark is upon it. There can be no mistaking. The North coast is riddled with his bitches, O'Connor. They try to turn a man from his natural duties. The thought of my natural heir conceived in my dearest wife maddens them. They howl to think upon divine right and divine righteousness."

What should an honest man say? I have been captain of my vessel this twenty year; I have sailed to the black shores of Crimea; I have traded with Berber canoes off the coast of Africa; I have seen the lights at the pole. Storms happen, and Neptune does not dally with witches. He has no need – his kingdom is more than half the world, or so the cartographers say.

So I said, "Aye, sir."

It was none of my business that the little princess began to laugh. It was a dark laugh, knowing, bitter.

They disembarked at Fife at a little after midday, and when they were gone I crossed myself without knowing why. That same night we made for Norway with a cargo of good produce, made smooth running across the North Sea, on, past Shetland, landing at Bergen under cover of night and with little fanfare.

God save the King.

***

Holyrood Palace, Edinburgh - 1579

Esme Stewart comes in like a trebuchet attack through an already-crumbling wall. In the night, in the middle of another waking hour, sixteen-year-old James wonders if, had his mother lived, had he ever met her or seen her face or felt her tenderness – and she would, surely have been tender? Surely maternal? Not a cold, backstairs assassin or blooded deer-hunter, surely, not to him – whether he might have been pure. Whether, had he been Catholic, he would have been pure. Sometimes he imagines kneeling to take the sacrament. Alongside his mother, perhaps in France, dappled by light through a stained-glass window, he pictures parting his lips to welcome the body of Christ. It is his most subversive fantasy, more so – far more so – than his other fantasies.

They would kill him.

His mother's lover killed his father and his cousin killed his mother.

Death is James's difficult sibling; inescapable, noisy. Very close.

Sometimes the fantasies collide. When he drifts half in and half out of dreams, there is a priest – not a cold, Calvinist priest who hates him, but a man in purple with incense, weaving smoke skeins that caress him – and the priest cups his chin and tips red wine, blood of Christ, very gently, onto his waiting tongue, and then follows with his lips: split and wet and hard and tender.

They would kill him for this too.

King James has never known himself not a king. At six months of age, still wailing wordlessly, he was anointed with holy oil and his fat infant hand placed upon the crown. One day, James will marry, and his son will be King of Scotland and the Islands: that much is already written, and he cannot unwrite that story. He wonders sometimes what he was before the coronation, and what he would have been without it. As a child he had longed to be a stable-boy, and had wandered into the royal stables whenever he evaded the grasp of his tutors. The boys were so tall and strong, with long limbs and a shamelessness about their own skin. But they flinched from him, and bowed their heads and mumbled "yer majesty" when he had passed, and he had tried to believe it was his rank that made them look away. In his small, sour heart, he had feared it was his pale ugliness that repelled them. If he had been red-haired and sturdy, would they have welcomed him?

Small King James had dragged his dark goblin self back up stone stairs and back to his books. The testaments did not flinch from him. They promised him the company of men who would open their arms to him in faith.

***

And so Esme Stewart, second cousin to the King, arrives in Edinburgh in a bleak midwinter. The snow does not cocoon the landscape in beauty. It comes down like furious exhalations from clouds that long to smother what lies beneath. Through the snow comes a man: his train is lavish, his horses fine, his woollen cape and riding cap deepest claret, flecked white with snow.

There should be a fanfare, James thinks, watching over the courtyard from an upper gallery where they permit him to walk. (Sixteen now, come to Edinburgh from Stirling to assume his personal rule, a monarch anointed by God himself, and he is allowed to walk from here to here, and no further, with permission doled out by bald men who preach sulphurous sermons with sulphurous breath: James pulls himself up to his full height and vows to use God's authority one day, like the judgement upon Sodom and Gomorrah, to scythe them all down along with their rules and their permissions and their galleries.) He tucks himself into a corner, out of the wind. One hand twines itself around a wooden finial.

Below, dusk and cacophony. Horses protest at being handled, and their kin in the stables answer them. Hoofs skitter on cobblestones. Grooms call between themselves, not unlike the horses, their cadences rising into the slow spirals of snow. Boys and serving women rush out of arched doorways flushed with light, spilling amber pools of it onto darkening stone, finding the baggage carts and beginning the slow and steady train of boxes that will find their ways down dark corridors and into private chambers.

In the centre of this vortex, very still, Esme Stewart. He has not dismounted. He gazes around him with a level equanimity. From his vantage point, James knows, and does not know how he knows, that the man enjoys these observations from height. Long-fingered hands draw his cape tightly around a slender frame. Beneath the claret cap is a fox-like countenance, beard sharp, lips curved. Amusement? Perhaps. The man has just arrived from France, from the court of the Guises themselves. He has left behind a wife and a clutch of children, it is said, to return to Scotland. From the time he was on the knee of his wet-nurse, James has heard stories of his mother's years in France. Even her Scots was spoken with a French accent, he has been told, this princess who became his mother, who would have been Queen of France. Even the boxes being unloaded from the wagons are branded with the tell-tale Fleur de Lys. Perhaps this French court gentleman is amused by the simplicity of this Holyrood yard, with its rough torches and horse shit on the flag stones. James allows himself to imagine the refinement his cousin is used to, and he longs to shrink back into himself until he is lost to shadows.

Then the man looks up towards the gallery. His eyes glitter in the amber light, and they meet James's eyes. There should be a fanfare, James thinks again. Some kind of explosion of silver and gold. Esme Stewart bows his head deeply, and pulls off his cap, and as his head rises again James sees red-gold hair, too long, shockingly womanly, suddenly studded all over with snowflakes. The boy king has been well taught. Lucifer was an angel, and beautiful in the eyes of God, he thinks. It feels like a memory, or a warning.

James is not given to running. Nevertheless, he runs.

Breathless, panting, horribly aware of the sweat on his brow and the flush in his cheeks, he stops at the foot of the stairs in the great entrance hall. He fumbles, all thumbs, at his collar and cuffs, for some reason anxious that they might be standing up in odd directions like quills on a porcupine. His palms itch. He could prickle quite out of his skin.

There are pendants all around. The unicorn, the phoenix, the stag rampant. They are all his colours. If I wanted to declare war, James thinks, they would mount them on pikes and carry them ahead of me. On my whim, unicorns and all.

In his hand, his trembling hand, lies the rich pearl he has prepared to welcome his guest.

When the great doors break open, and a man steps through the space, and a cold wind breaks like a wave over him, James Stuart grins like a child.

Demon Rock

By Gabriel Wisdom

What follows is a first-hand account of events which occurred eleven years ago. Due to the odd nature of this testimony, authorization to publish was only granted posthumously, as specified in the last will and testament of Doctor Mary Hightower. She was a highly respected psychologist, whose reputation was beyond reproach. This is a factual written account of events as witnessed, without analysis or interpretation.

Across the Inland Empire's desert communities, a large rumbling sound was heard in the pre-dawn hours on February 21, 2000. Initial reports suggested an earthquake, even though none was detected by monitoring stations. The source of the disturbance did, in fact, come from Landers, California, where eight years prior a 7.3 magnitude earthquake had shaken the region, and tremors had been felt as far away as Arizona, Las Vegas, and Boise, Idaho.

The actual cause of the February 2000 rumble was discovered several days later by tourists. To their surprise, the famous twenty-five-thousand-pound boulder known as 'Giant Rock' had split in two.

There were a variety of explanations put forward. Some said the break was caused by geomagnetic disturbances underground. Giant Rock's location is described as an energy vortex of naturally occurring electrical currents.

In 1937, an eccentric German spy tunneled underneath the giant rock and built his subterranean home. The FBI tried to coax him out in 1942, but he killed himself by lighting a stick of dynamite. Some said the explosion is what initially started the break.

The cavern's next occupant was a test-pilot for Howard Hughes. Over a twenty-year span, he hosted UFO conventions at the site, and designed a static electric-powered longevity machine which, to this day, is housed under a nearby dome. There is speculation that Giant Rock was split by escaping energy from the vortex.

The background I've just described has been corroborated and published. Beyond this, local lore is filled with unsubstantiated accounts of ancestral Indian tribes who conducted spiritual ceremonies during which only the Chief was allowed to touch the rock. Another widely circulated tale involves a Hopi shaman who, in 1927, reportedly said that the future of the 21st century would be foretold by how Giant Rock cracked.

Likewise, there will be skeptics who ask why we hadn't come forward earlier...

Mary Hightower suffered from chronic obstructive pulmonary disease. Immediately following what I am now authorized to disclose, Mary enjoyed excellent health. When she gave her physician a detailed account of events, he surprised her by refusing further care on the basis that it was antithetical to his personal beliefs. Consequently, to preserve her good reputation, and mine as well, we determined the story was indeed strange and too perplexing to publish, until now.

***

It was two o'clock, on February 20, 2000. Bagging groceries

was mindless work, and for me it was humiliating. My career as a newspaper columnist had ended when the paper had folded, another victim of the internet. I checked the clock – still one more hour left. My mind wandered, and I thought about the travel brochure I'd picked up for Thai-Asia Airlines: 'Cheap enough to say, Phuket, I'll go.'

'Would you like some help carrying out your groceries?' Randy the cashier asked. She'd been a checker at King's since I was a kid.

'No, I'm good,' an attractive young woman said rolling her cart forward. She ignored me. I was used to it. Nobody pays much attention to the bagger. I sighed, taking another look at the time. Fifty-seven minutes left. 'Phuket, I'll go...'

'Adrian Bolt, is that you?' Almost instantly, I recognized the voice of Doctor Mary Hightower, the psychologist and guidance counselor from my old high school.

'Oh, hi, Doctor Mary!' Everyone called her that. 'Ah, nice to see you,' I said, trying to look like I hadn't noticed the nasal cannula attached to her face, and a silver oxygen tank on wheels.

'Paper or plastic?' Randy the cashier asked.

'Paper bags, dear,' she said, turning to me. 'I've seen your byline in the Joshua Tree Times. You're a good reporter. I didn't know you wanted to be a writer. Doesn't pay much, I suppose,' Hightower wheezed.

'I'm at Coachella College. I graduate next year, and then I'd like to write full-time.' I didn't know what else to say. Doctor Mary's order was heavy, so I double-bagged, and then placed them in the cart.

'Would you like some help out?' Randy posed the standard refrain. There aren't many ways you can ask the same question, day after day.

'Adrian here will help me. Is that okay with you, Mr. Bolt?' Doctor Mary hadn't changed, except that she was old. Cart in tow, I followed her out to the parking area.

When the last of the bags was loaded, and I'd closed the trunk, she handed me a tip. 'Thanks,' I said, and stuffed the bill into a pocket without looking.

'Adrian Bolt.' Mary let the words settle. 'That's a good name for a writer, or a business man.' In high school, I'd spent a lot of time in her office. 'Your personality assessment indicated you've got a good head for business.' Her blue-gray eyes reflected the late afternoon sun. 'If you're going to write,' she said, 'you'll need to find an intriguing story. Something to remind people that there are greater forces in the universe than the internet.'

'Huh, huh,' was all I could muster. I'd been a successful columnist, and now I was working in a grocery store. Considering the agony, and the embarrassment, I hoped Doctor Mary wasn't disappointed. It was good to see her.

'You ever hear about that place they call Giant Rock?' she asked me. 'There's a colorful history there. Some people claim it's magical. She coughed, and touched my shoulder to steady herself.

'Are you alright, Doctor Mary?' I was genuinely concerned. My parents had been killed on my eighteenth birthday. A long story short, Doctor Mary had taken an interest. Hell, she'd probably saved my life.

'I'm fine,' she spluttered, clearing her throat. 'Give me a call sometime, Adrian, and I'll fill you in. That's the world's largest free-standing boulder, you know. I'm in the phone book.' She chuckled gently, and closed the car door.

Walking back to the check-out aisle, I pulled the bill from my pocket, wondering how much of a tip she'd given. It was a hundred dollars! That had to be a record at King's. Certainly for baggers, I thought, proudly. After work, I planned to call and thank her.

***

Three o'clock and I was free at last. My vintage VW Bug had a squeaky door and, closing it, I had to be careful not to pull off the badly cracked plastic handle. Then I used a big clunky cell phone the newspaper had told me to keep. On the sixth ring, she picked up.

'Doctor Hightower,' she answered, clearing her throat.

'Hi, Doctor Mary. It's Adrian Bolt.'

'Oh yes, yes.' She sounded pleased.

'Are you sure that tip was supposed to be a hundred, instead of ten dollars?' I felt a bit shy.

'Oh yes,' she repeated. 'Figured you might know better than me what to do with the money. Hang on a minute. Let me sit down.'

I could hear her breathing. Then she groaned. 'I'm here.'

'Well, thank you, Doctor Mary. I sure do appreciate your generosity. It was nice seeing you.'

'Listen, son, if you've got time right now, why don't you come by my place? Giant Rock is a fifteen minute drive from here.'

'Sure, I'll come over if you think it's a good idea.'

'You want to be writer, so try this on. Supposedly, the boulder is in an energy vortex. Fifty years ago, people slept on the ground out there, hoping to cure all kinds of maladies. You could do an investigative report. Who knows, but I do think it makes for an interesting story. And there's a little cave house under the boulder that was occupied by a German spy who blew himself up in that hole to avoid being captured. Then a friend of his moved in, and more crazy things went on after that. I'll fill you in.'

'On my way,' I said. When I turned the ignition, the horn blared, and the head lamps were blinking in time with the beeping horn. Customers stopped to see what was going on. There was a breaker re-set switch under the glove box, and that did the trick. Then I pulled out, heading towards Landers, thinking, 'Phuket, I'll go.'

***

It was the last house on a shaded acre of palm trees and desert tamarisk. I pulled into the driveway, and walked up to a freshly painted green door. The front window was partially open.

I called out, 'Doctor Mary! It's Adrian.'

She answered from a covered pavilion in the side yard. 'I'm over here.' Until a couple of hours earlier, I hadn't seen her in ten years. I wanted to help her to the car, but she insisted on carrying her oxygen tank.

'I brought sandwiches and a couple of waters. You like turkey?' she asked, handing over the brown bag.

'Yeah, I'm starving,' I said, eyeing the bag. I hadn't eaten since breakfast.

Mary explained there wasn't enough lettuce growing in her garden, so she'd decided to use nasturtiums. 'Orange flowers with a slightly peppery taste reminiscent of watercress,' she told me. 'Good herbal medicine, packed with vitamin C, and lutein.'

We strapped in, and then I turned the ignition. Mary seemed amused when I had to disable the honking horn. We headed south on Kuna Avenue, towards Giant Rock Road, where it snaked along the darkening foothills of Spy Mountain. The afternoon sun had already passed to the windward side as we left the paved portion for the graded dirt road. It was bumpy, and I was forced to slow down.

'There it is,' Mary said, pointing to a sparse habitat in the distance.

The world's largest boulder was hiding somewhere in what looked like the bottom of a dry sea bed.

'This was the epicenter of the largest California earthquake in fifty years. That was eight years ago -- you remember?' Mary's hand pointed to a long ditch. I could see where the earth had been forced open and stitched back at the seams.

'That was a big one, 7.2 on the Richter Scale,' I said, talking over the road noise. 'The Landers earthquake gave geologists some new insights on how it triggered sympathetic quakes in Nevada and Wyoming, and other faults all the way down to the Gulf of Mexico.' I'd written several pieces for the newspaper back then, and still recalled the relevant details. Mary seemed pleased.

We passed by the tectonic plate rupture lines, and there it was. What I'd mistaken for a mountain turned out to be the biggest rock I'd ever seen. I understood why it was called Giant Rock. We parked in between Spy Mountain and the gigantic boulder.

Mary gestured towards a wind break at the base of the rock. 'We can eat lunch over there.' A brisk wind was carrying little bits of sand, and her spot offered some shelter. A plant was growing in the crags. It had white trumpet-shaped flowers with pointed petals that wrapped like half-folded umbrellas. We sat there, and began eating our sandwiches.

'This is where a German immigrant named Frank Critzer set up camp here in 1931. He filed a mining claim, and then he began to blast out a 24 by 36 foot, two-room home underneath this rock. He created a ventilated living room, kitchen, and a bedroom, and there was a window at the top of these stairs.' Hightower pointed to a burnt metal rectangle laying on the ground. 'That might be his front door,' she said.

I was trying to take notes.

'Don't worry about writing any of this down,' Mary told me. 'We can do that later. Okay, so Critzer graded a landing strip on the dry lakebed over there,' she gestured. 'And he installed a short-wave radio antenna on that other rock. He claimed his body was so full of electricity that he could charge the batteries just by putting them under his pillow while he slept.'

I was enthralled, and having a great time.

'Well,' Mary said, clasping her hands, 'Critzer had been under FBI investigation for suspicious activities. They thought he was a Nazi spy and, in 1942, at the height of war paranoia, three Riverside deputy sheriffs tried to coax him from the cave by throwing flares through the window. One of the flares landed on a box of dynamite stored in his living room. Critzer used the flare to light one of the wicks, and he was blown to hell, right here, under this rock.'

We got up for a closer look into the blast-hole, leaving the sandwiches by the white trumpet-shaped flowers. Two stone steps led down into the crevice. It wasn't wide enough to squeeze through and I started feeling claustrophobic. It was creepy down in the hollow. I walked back up, and found the wind had blown the tips of the white flowers over our sandwiches. Doctor Mary was holding onto the side, and I watched as she made her way up. Then I brushed the flowers away and handed one sandwich to her. Then I grabbed mine and wolfed it down.

'After the German spy, what happened?' I guess I'd mumbled through a mouthful because I got a disapproving look from her.

Mary finished another bite, and washed it down with a swallow of water. 'They never determined if Critzer was actually a spy,' she said. 'Any evidence there might have been was destroyed in the explosion. He had a friend -- a test pilot working for Hughes Aircraft in Los Angeles named George Van Tassel. After hearing about Critzer, Van Tassel flew out here with his boss, Howard Hughes. They landed on the dry lakebed airstrip nearby.' She finished eating and looked over at me. 'Taste good?' she asked.

'Just right, thanks,' I answered. I didn't mention the bitter taste of the seeds, or whatever they were.

'Mine was a little bitter,' Mary confessed. 'Next time, I'll go lighter on the nasturtiums. They're supposed be peppery, not bitter.' She shrugged and continued the story. 'Howard Hughes lost his mind. You probably know this.'

'Yup, the L.A. Times says that Warner Brothers and Disney have plans for a movie with Leo DiCaprio. He's cast to play lead as Howard Hughes.'

'Some of it is to be filmed out here. San Bernardino, I think.' Mary swept her white braided hair to the side. 'Hughes would go three or four days without sleep, and on top of that he had a serious germ phobia. Sometimes he'd burn all his clothes just to kill what he couldn't see. Nobody wanted to call him crazy, maybe because he was the richest person in the world.'

Wheezing again, she paused to catch her breath. I offered to bring the oxygen canister from the VW but she waved me away. Then, after a deep inhale, and blowing the air out with dogged determination, she continued.

'George Van Tassel rebuilt that cave-home under the rock, and lived here for twenty years. After he claimed he'd been taken aboard a UFO, Van Tassel began hosting the Giant Rock UFO Conventions, which attracted large crowds. To feed them, his wife opened a café, called the COME ON INN, ha!' Mary let out a belly laugh.

The winds were calm in the golden light just before sunset, and I imagined being there sixty or seventy years ago during those UFO gatherings. 'At the grocery store, did you say people continue to believe this place is magical?' I asked.

'That's right,' she said. 'Supposedly, this was Indian holy ground, dating back to pre-history. Shamans and Medicine Men,' she paused, 'and Medicine Women met with Chiefs of the east and west tribes. They all gathered here for healing. So, when Van Tassel began speaking and writing about extending the human lifespan with static electricity from the ground, it got a lot of media attention. According to him, the secret to a long life was to recharge your cells with the earth's natural electromagnetism, which he compared to charging a car battery.'

'Do you think any of what Van Tassel claimed is true? I mean, the idea of recharging the human body?'

She raised an eyebrow. 'Maybe some of it is. The rocks here contain metallic minerals, and when the ground water percolates, it creates a natural battery. If an electrical current flows through the ore in this boulder, people might feel something. But I don't think there's any scientific evidence to support Van Tassel's ideas about recharging your cells for longevity.'

As I listened to what Doctor Mary was saying, I realized how special she was.

'For years,' she said, 'scientists have thought about transforming human body-heat into electricity. Even when we're sleeping, our bodies produce about a hundred watts of power. During waking hours, the average person produces three to four hundred watts. If you're moving quickly, your body's electrical output is about two thousand watts. You and I have as much energy stored in our fat cells as a one-ton battery.'

My attention was drawn to the kaleidoscopic colors of the darkening sky. Strange geometric patterns swirled about. I reached up, trying to touch one, and the images trailed from my arm. Doctor Mary was talking, but I couldn't understand what she was saying. Her words seem to float momentarily, and disappeared like little clouds. My mind raced and I wondered what was happening. When I looked at Mary, her large black pupils were like constellations of stars.

'Adrian, I feel funny,' she said. I thought her voice sounded like music.

'Giant Rock is alive,' I told her. 'See? It's breathing.' I placed my hand on the rock, and thought I heard laughter coming from the white trumpet-shaped flowers with pointed petals that wrapped like half-folded umbrellas.

Mary was staring at the flowers. 'Adrian,' she said firmly, gesturing with her hand, 'this is Jimson Weed, a genus of Belladonna.' She wasn't smiling. 'Datura Stramonium, known by the common names Thorn Apple, Mad Apple, Angel's Trumpet, and Devil's Snare, among others. The seeds and petals are psychoactive entheogens. If you inhale or eat any part of the plant,' Mary said looking away, 'you'll have visions, hallucinations. These plants were used by native shamans for religious and magical rituals. Amounts needed to produce the effect are very small. Slightly higher amounts can be lethal.'

She looked up, and suddenly I felt the electric grip of fear. I tried to speak, but there was a dry choking at my throat.

'Adrian,' Mary declared in between labored breaths. 'I'm afraid we both ate whatever came off of those flowers – seeds, maybe. You know, the bitter taste?' Her jaw tightened visibly. 'I've heard the trip lasts nine hours, sometimes longer. Can you drive?' The deepening worry lines across her forehead gave me pause.

I turned to look at the car, and everything was melting into the golden twilight. 'I don't think so, no. I shouldn't drive,' I thought, still unable to speak. I decided to look around.

***

Even at a steady stride, I had no idea how long it took getting to the other side of the boulder. I was alerted by a sharp, desperate cry. Several seconds of silence passed before I heard it again, this time louder and more painful than the last. I guessed it had to be a tortured animal somewhere beyond the fading light. My heart beat quickly. Suddenly, one black shadow seemed to run from another, and then something stabbed me in the chest. Panic stricken, I turned full circle, looking up. The night was calm and clear, and the stars shivered in the yellow brilliance of the Milky Way.

I told myself, these are hallucinations, mere creations of my imagination. There was another series of screams and cries, as if all the pain in the world had found a voice. A twig or something snapped behind me, and I turned, but saw nothing except for Joshua trees and high desert scrub. A movement near Giant Rock caught my attention. I followed the silhouette. It was a horned creature running on two legs down a bushy slope.

I watched as it raced to the top of the boulder on all fours, steadying itself with a pair of large translucent wings. The half-bestial creature began to howl from the high ledge. It was a piercing, tortured wail. With every breath, I felt the heavy beat of my heart.

A sprinkle of lights shone on the luminous horizon, indicating the desert town several miles away. Fear surged through my body like a current, and I began to run towards the lights, stopping only to catch my breath. Every dark form in the dim starlight seemed ominous. Something moved. I froze, hearing nothing but the sounds of my own blood pulsing in my ears. Yet something was coming, creeping up on me, I was sure of it.

There was a crazy sounding laugh, and the apparition howled again, this time more painfully. I turned towards the cries, then I pivoted, and began running at full speed in the opposite direction until I was out of earshot. The world was blurred as I pressed on. I was frightened. Any thoughts of a return to Giant Rock and Doctor Mary were overtaken by all that the darkness might conceal.

Realizing I was lost, I stopped to get some bearings. Then I turned around, and began to walk intently, trying to retrace my steps. Spy Mountain rose against the silhouetted horizon, and I shuddered at the thought of being forced to spend the night among the unknown dangers of the desert jungle. My only chance was to face the awful apparition. I picked up the pace, weaving between spiny ocotillo bushes and the shrubby undergrowth, while keeping an eye on the faint outline of Giant Rock.

Without warning, the demon leaped from the blue shadows, running past me on all-fours. There was whooping and grunting, and a flash of fire in the eyes. The great colorless bat wings fluttered, and the thing vanished in a gust of sour winds. I tried to see where it had gone, and then the creature cried out in strained words.

'Have you come to torture us?' the voices echoed. It was a guttural harsh growling sound, unlike anything I'd ever heard from an ordinary animal.

I couldn't see the demon, but thought I sensed it from beneath the red patch of earth under me.

'Have you come to punish us?' cried the disembodied voices.

'No!' I shouted, trembling as I strained to find the demon.

'Have you come to unchain us, to free us from the rock?'

The words swirled like a dust devil. I was being drawn to the ground by some magnetic force.

'Yes, yes,' I shouted. 'I've come to free you.'

The creature appeared again from the shadows. This time it hovered above me, glaring down with two sets of eyes that blazed like fire. I heard the demon whisper something in a jumble of disjointed words. There was a terrible, familiar smell, like the trumpet-shaped flowers we'd accidently eaten – and Doctor Mary – was she having the same terrible visions, I wondered. My eyes were fixed on the inky silhouette above as it turned to smoke.

The north wind had picked up. It was pushing me towards the outline of Spy Mountain. Everything else had melted into blackness, and all color seemed to have vanished from the world. As the last of my strength suddenly slipped away, I sat on the ground to rest.

I thought about those flowers… Jimsonweed, Mad Apple, Angel's trumpet, Devil's Snare. Mary had said the local Indians used them for religious and magic rituals. I closed my eyes, listening to the hypnotic tom-tom beating of my heart. I remember dreaming of an old shaman holding a basket of flowers. 'Eat a little, and go to sleep,' the Indian said. 'Eat more, and dream. Eat a lot and never wake up.'

***

The morning breezes were pleasant in the pre-dawn light. There was a loud rumbling sound, and disjointed memories and impressions of the things that had happened overnight. I rose slowly from the dry creek, and saw the giant boulder moving up and down and from side to side, with rapid, forceful, jerky motions, until a long vertical crack appeared like a flesh wound. The Giant Rock began to bleed, slowly at first, then at a steady pulse. I rubbed my eyes, as the escaping ooze combusted. Fire and black smoke rose from the boulder, creating a thick darkness in the sky, and the demonic shape of horns and blood-curdling bat wings were made visible by the presence of the escaping vapors. My eyes burned. I closed them, and my nostrils flared with the awful smell of escaping sewer gas.

All at once, the rumbling ended. When I looked, Giant Rock had split in half. Then I remembered: Doctor Mary! Panicking, I ran to the boulder, now in two large sections.

'Doctor Mary, where are you? Doctor Mary, Doctor Mary!' I shouted, with a hoarse phlegm in my throat. My chest tightened as I walked to where Critzer and Van Tassel had once lived and died. Our wind-break and the white trumpet-shaped flowers lay buried in a pile of rubble. My heart raced.

'Over here, Adrian,' Doctor Mary called out. She was sitting on the ground. 'You okay?'

Relieved, I waved frantically. 'I'm good. Be right there,' I answered, half-running towards her. To my amazement, she jumped to her feet, smiling. We stood there, holding each other, knowing we'd shared something unspeakable. I noticed her breathing sounded unobstructed and clear. Then we walked silently to the VW Bug, and got in. When I turned the ignition, the sounds of the honking horn felt comfortable, like the feeling of being home after a long journey. I pushed the re-set breaker switch, and we drove away. Neither of us spoke. We didn't need to.

***

Mary enjoyed good health in the years that followed. We met for lunch every Wednesday, and she helped me find a job as a travel writer. When I was comped by various resorts and travel destinations, she came along. Last year, sadly, we lost her. After the funeral, I received a call from her lawyer, asking me to come in for a reading of the will.

Vaughn Crowley had been Mary's attorney the past forty years. He explained: 'Doctor Hightower's estate owns a stock portfolio valued at nine point three million dollars, plus seven-hundred thousand in a savings and checking account. Recently, she purchased King's Grocery enterprise, and the building it occupies.' There were other assets which he listed. Then Crowley read from the letter.

'Being of sound mind and body, I bequeath all worldly possessions to Adrian Bolt, my good friend and a blossoming writer. Now you have the freedom to tell our story. See you on the other side.' It was signed, 'Your Partner in Time, Mary Hightower.'

I readily admitted to assisting her suicide. Everyone at home knew what I'd done. But, as they say, 'What everybody knows isn't worth knowing.' The truth is that we'd gone and visited Giant Rock again, for old times' sake, just a year ago. That was when the damned demon had reappeared and, this time, had become trapped in her lungs. Her time had finally been up, her misery had been unspeakable, and she'd begged me to help. I've been handling her affairs from my prison cell at the California Men's Colony in San Luis Obispo ever since.

The Demon in the Mirror

By Elyn Joy

On a warm June night, a decade or so ago, a dead man stood on this very flower-lined path, pleading with the caterer to help him find his wife. The gardens had been closed for over an hour; still, Eliot had no reason to suspect that the man was dead. Sure, he looked a bit dated—not to mention off-season—in his attire, given the heavy tweed suit and top hat; yet, otherwise, he seemed perfectly real. In fact, the man's cigar sent curls of white smoke so sweetly fragrant, they overpowered even the headiest of jasmine blooms and caused the caterer's eyes to water.

Eliot stood beneath a string of twinkle lights and called his manager to report that an elderly gentleman had lost his wife. The garden staff sprung to it and, soon enough, a legion of white-shirted, red-bow-tied catering folk were combing the cobbled trails. Meanwhile, the man continued to pace back and forth in shiny black shoes, muttering woefully. Having initiated the search, Eliot hollered out to him.

'Don't worry, sir; we've got people searching. If your wife is here, we'll find her.'

'No, no, she's *not* here!' the man howled.

'Where was she when you last saw her?'

The poor fellow was practically hysterical. 'Right here.' He pointed down at a bed of purple irises.

'Right where?'

'There. She's been six feet under for a hundred years… but now she's gone! We're *all* gone!'

Eliot glanced at the window of the Whitman Gardens wedding hall, hoping someone else may have heard this madness. The lights were off, and in the darkened window Eliot saw a reflection of himself and a brightly glowing, top-hatted figure in a tweed suit. The ghastly thing's skin appeared translucent—almost nonexistent—the face more skull-like than human. Alarmed, he stepped back, tripping over his catering cart, and falling hard on the gravel. And when he looked up, the man was gone.

No sign of the mysterious visitor was seen again, but garden-goers have since reported the aroma of sweet cigar smoke drifting down the lush pathways on many a warm night.

But how rude of me; I almost forgot to introduce myself. I'm Louise Montclair, scientist and paranormal interpreter. I know, it sounds a bit of a contradiction. But it's rather simple, really: by training, I'm a biolinguistic decoder (one who deciphers natural communication systems). Yet, due to the events of the very night I mentioned, I've learned that, while some messages lack words or even symbols, others push and push on the walls of the psyche until at last they find their course.

Such a tale was sprung from that evening. I'd been at the gardens for a fellow lab doctor's wedding. Having tired of socializing, my colleagues Anne and Henry suggested that we sneak away for a private toast at Monet's Pond (an area strictly prohibited after hours). We sidestepped security through the back gate, giggling like delinquent high-schoolers down the shadowed brick path to the sparkling, lily-pad-dotted water.

We sat by the edge, toasting the crickets' rhythmic chant, a nice respite from the DJ's dance tracks. Naturally, we got on the topic of our recent project exploring the 'language' of trees in a forest, marveling at how they do converse—only in slow-time. For instance, an oak might send out a message of danger—say, an encroaching disease or predatorial insect—and, eventually, that maple a hundred yards away (along with all those in between) will begin developing a stronger root system, or a thicker layer of bark, and all in response to a warning relayed from across the grove.

We were imagining the 'conversations' among those silvery aspens across the pond when we heard voices rising from the prairie path.

'If she has dementia, she may have wandered into the water!' a low voice called.

Who were they looking for? Me? Anne? Flickering flashlights scanned the far shoreline.

'We'd better move, guys—maybe pretend we got lost?' Henry suggested. 'Louise, what do you think?'

The voices were nearing, but something had caught my eye… so I didn't move. At first I thought it was the passing reflection of a bird overhead—perhaps a pond duck, or maybe a bat? Yet something else had formed on the water's surface—a shape I'd mistaken for the wavy-mirrored moon.

Could it really be… a face? Impossible, I thought, passing it off as one of those lucky koi fish looking for a midnight snack.

'Louise? Come on, already!'

'Go on—I'll catch up!'

The lights were closer now; one skimmed the reeds just a few feet to my right.

I stood to go, then stopped.

The milky oval had returned, this time bearing the distinctive features of a woman's face. It was as though she had ascended a staircase from the pond's bottom and now stood on the other side of a strange, starlit mirror. Her hair was coiffed as if perfectly dry, the toffee-hued bun adorned with flowers. She wore a mint-green gown, plainly visible beneath the soggy brown eyes and pale neck. She had a lamp-like, shimmering radiance, much like a bioluminescent sea creature.

Breathless, I stepped back, yet felt compelled to stay. My intuition told me to touch the water. *Touch the water, touch the water,* the feeling insisted.

My knees dropped. The rustling behind me seemed miles away as I balanced myself on the wet shore. I reached for the cold surface; within seconds my arm burned as though it had been pricked by a thousand needles. Somehow, I sensed no harm was intended and managed to remain calm. Although her lips never moved, I could 'hear' the vision's words in a soft, floating voice.

'Up on the north hill at Fairmount… tell him. Tell them. Find me.'

I pulled away just as the tall grass parted. Squinting against the light, I could make out four white shirts.

'By chance, have you lost your husband, ma'am?' I glanced back; the dark water stood silent, although my arm was still on fire.

I replied with a dazed *no*—claiming that I'd taken a wrong turn from the wedding. Once they informed me about the distraught gentleman up front, I had to wonder if the two incidents had been connected. While I tried to pass off my encounter as a wine-induced hallucination, I also knew what I'd seen. As for what I thought I'd heard, science couldn't rule out its plausibility. Water, like most of nature, is remarkably intelligent, able to carry information over vast distances—even from one generation to the next. Had the water at Monet's Pond 'spoken' to me? And, if so, whose message had it conveyed, and why? These questions became my private quest. You see, as a scientist, I have to protect my reputation.

So I kept my secret—that is, until around Halloween time when, in America anyway, ghost stories please crowds and sell papers. My friend Anne directed me to *The Denver Post*, specifically to an article titled 'Local Spirit Tells of Love After Death'. It spoke of how, before the western prairie had been claimed by the city, the entire Whitman Gardens area had been a makeshift, 'free for all' burial ground for natives and early settlers. When developers began their pursuit of 'progress' in the mid-1920's, countless human remains had been unearthed. Among these were the handsomely-dressed bones of a male and a female… who, in the rush to relocate the dead, had been separated. The article continued:

> 'Yet, last June, an alleged apparition manifested at the precise location where, a century ago, the couple's bones had been excavated. The sole witness, a wedding caterer named Eliot, provided first-hand testimony which matched the spirit's description to the area's original landowner, Mr. Charles Whitman—long thought to have been cremated. Spurred by the sighting, investigators used GPR (ground-penetrating radar) to explore the possibility of Whitman's ill-directed burial. His since-verified remains were later discovered in an unmarked site at the nearby Settler's Cemetery. Plans are underway to relocate Whitman to the grand west entrance of his namesake gardens. Meanwhile, the search continues for Mrs. Whitman. If anyone has information, please contact *The Denver Post* at the number below.'

Let me repeat: I'm a scientist, not a 'woo woo' person. Still, I felt it my duty to relay my experience—just in case my imploring pond-messenger *had* been the grieving ghost's wife after all. I rang the number and reported the full encounter: the woman, the water, even the needle-like marks on my arm that had lasted a week. Within a few days, the news broke: the undertaker at Fairmount Cemetery had found two 'unknown female' graves on the north hill—both from the time in question. Happily, the first one to be exhumed was the body of Iris Whitman, beloved wife of the late Charles Whitman. The story described how she'd been identified in part by her signature mint-green ball gown, along with hair and dental samples, all thanks to an anonymous tip. The couple had been reunited, and an upcoming ceremony would mark the occasion.

The paper's editor called me the next day. He asked that I reconsider my anonymity and appear in a feature story. After a day's consideration, I accepted, hoping to generate greater public interest in the unseen aspects of science—always a challenge in my field. 'Louise Montclair: Denver's Talented Paranormal Scientist' made waves, first locally, and then nationally. The requests poured in—and, before long, I was invited to 'interpret' everything from a haunted church in Kansas to a bar-hopping orb in Chicago.

I was surprised at the similarities between this work and my other research, in that most paranormal events turn out to be quite natural. When I say 'natural', I don't mean ordinary; rather, I mean 'nature-connected'. I've since come to realize that Nature is neither good nor evil; rather, it is *indifferent.* It follows the universal law of cause and effect, much like a mirror reflects—as long, that is, as humans, the world's most expert deflectors, don't interfere.

***

But let's move on, shall we?—to the house on 969 Spruce Street, the place that both challenged and reaffirmed my most confident understandings about science. It's just over there, beyond the old Whitman Manor and down that quaint, tree-lined street.

Hear those blackbirds? They love days like this, when the sun is still gentle, and the first worms of spring lie just beneath the new grass. In my first research job, our team deciphered over a hundred 'words' in blackbird-ese, but science tells us the real number may be five hundred or more. I often wonder when I hear them—might they be philosophizing? Gossiping? Spouting poetry? One thing is certain: like everyone and everything else, they are expressing *something*.

Ah, here it is… 969. I know this house well—but how changed it looks, with its sunny, white-painted stone and blue-shuttered windows. Back then, the place seemed steeped in gray, like a soggy old sepia photo. I'll never forget that dreary Wednesday—almost a year after the Whitman Gardens sightings—when this strange chapter began.

I'd been in my lab, studying the chemical messages relayed among rock formations (think slow time, only slower), when a woman called me in a panic. She'd seen me on the news a few months back and was desperate for help; she rambled nonsensically about rats and cracks and a cursed statue. Given my schedule, I hesitated… but, out of curiosity, I agreed to stop by on my way home.

A clammy mist had settled in when I first knocked on that weather-worn door—nothing like the elegant red one you see now.

'Hello?' The woman's wide grey eyes popped through the small peephole-grate. Her voice was raspy, as though she'd been shouting for a long while. 'Are you Louise? Louise Montclair?'

'I am.'

The peephole closed; the door opened into a shabby foyer with dull, peeling wallpaper.

'Come in.'

The woman may have been in her thirties, but it was hard to say, since she had the gaunt, faded appearance of someone decades older. Her red hair—by far the most colorful thing about her—hung in unruly strings against her pale cheeks. She wore a blue wrap dress with scuffed brown shoes. *Very retro,* I thought. She scanned my attire with an odd expression (I wore jeans and a gray pullover). I wondered whether I should have dressed more professionally.

'I'm Etta,' she finally said. 'I do appreciate your coming from so far away.'

'Oh, it wasn't far at all. I work just down at the university.'

She nodded blankly, and we chatted briefly about the weather, the garden, and her son's interest in hunting—a topic spurred by the bewildering presence of an antique rifle blocking the hallway. Etta offered me a cup of tea and a seat at a rickety wooden table, after clearing away what looked like a bloody, half-eaten steak on a rusted dish.

'Sugar?'

Her speech felt formal, almost out of touch—yet I've always had a soft spot for eccentrics.

'No, thank you.'

I shuffled in the rickety chair, mentally fidgeting with my own growing apprehension. I couldn't quite name what was nagging at me, at least not yet. Maybe it was the too-loud *tick, tick, tick* of the deer head clock (yes, antlers and all) looming over the table… or the bleak grayness of the room, or the overpowering smell of mold… I think it was all of these, but something else, too. I noticed a dead plant in the corner, and the answer came: despite all its apparent activity, the place felt lifeless. This confused me, since Etta seemed so pleasant.

THUD.

'Sorry about the flies!' Etta had smashed an unlucky one with her bare hand. She flicked it off the tabletop like a crumb.

'How long have you lived here?' I asked, averting my eyes from the dark smear.

'Quite a long time now.'

I started to ask specifics, when a door slammed above us. Next came the clonk of descending footsteps. A tall, dirty-blonde-haired boy of around fifteen emerged from the back hallway. He wore a stained white shirt and dull green work pants. He brushed past Etta and me, sullen-faced and silent.

'Joey? Say hello to our guest.'

The boy neither blinked nor turned to acknowledge us. He strode to the small refrigerator and removed what looked and smelled like a raw fish.

'Joseph, don't be rude. Louise here is going to help us with the house... and the *statue*.'

The boy chuckled softly, his close-cut hair glinting like a bed of needles, his pointy face sickly beneath the green-toned bulb.

'That's funny,' he sneered.

He plunked the odorous thing onto a plate, slung the rifle over his shoulder, then disappeared behind the cracked wall. A heavy silence simmered beneath the tick of the deer clock.

'Oh no… I'm terribly sorry...' Etta hunched forward and sobbed, her bony shoulders quaking. I tried to comfort her as she whimpered like a wounded dog, relaying the torment she'd endured ever since her husband had died.

'Lately, things have grown unbearable,' she cried.

'What sorts of things?' I asked gently.

'Oh, so many. It's felt like a century since anything was normal. Just last week, the winds almost dashed me away... ' her voice trailed as she hugged her body.

'Winds? Outside?'

She shook her head. 'No, inside.'

'You mean air-conditioning?'

'Conditioning?'

She then recounted an evening when, while she'd been working on her fur quilt (I didn't ask), a sudden gust had blindsided her. It blew the soup off the stove, caused her to stab her own hand with the quilting needle, and left her crawling through a seeming hurricane to get to the stairs. When she'd finally reached Joey's room, she'd found him quietly pinning live beetles to a board. His curtains hadn't moved a flutter, although his window had been propped open. Bewildered, she'd run back downstairs to find an uncanny stillness, along with a jumbled mess.

'It took me three hours to straighten it out, and three more to stop shaking,' she wailed.

'How strange.' I can't say I believed her. She seemed so fragile, maybe vitamin-deficient and sleep-deprived, too. 'Anything else?'

'Oh, yes. Let's see… there are the screams—beast-like shrieks that wake us at all hours… and then the rats jumping out from the drains every day. Joey has dropped poison in every one of them, but do you think that stops them?'

'I would think it might help.'

'Oh, and I almost forgot the root.'

'The root? A tree root?'

Etta choked back a sob, holding her neck as she described how a root had popped up from the basement drain last month. At first, she'd ignored it, but it had kept twisting higher… and then last week, it had tried to strangle her by the clothesline. 'Every tree on the property will be chopped down and ripped out tomorrow, and all the pipes will be scoured out, too.' She sat up with sudden assurance.

'This all sounds terribly upsetting… and surreal… '

'Yes, but what I need help with most, Louise, is the statue. She's destroying my sweet Joey. I hardly recognize him anymore.'

'Statue? Go on.' I glanced around the room but saw nothing resembling a statue.

Etta stood and began pacing near the dirty window.

'It's all her fault. Everything. I can take the rest, but not what she's done to Joey. You saw it yourself—he's rude and angry all the time… and he's *mean.* Just yesterday, I saw him grab a tiny rabbit from the back stoop and crush it in his own hand. And when I scolded him, he denied it had ever happened.' Etta met my gaze with her sad, red-rimmed eyes. 'He laughed, Miss Montclair. *Laughed.* Please, help us... '

'Listen, Etta—I'm not sure... but I'd like to see this statue.

May I?'

'Of course.'

Etta's dress sagged on her gaunt frame as she led me to a water-stained back hallway that reeked of mildew. Besides the dreadful clock, the only decorative item I'd seen in the house was the gold-framed black-and-white photo hanging in this darkened corridor. I wanted to stop and study it, but the light was dim, and Etta rushed on. We passed a steep, narrow stairway leading up to the second floor, and another leading down to a dungeon-like abyss.

'That's the laundry. But the root's still in there, so I can't… '

'Don't worry, Etta,' I patted her shoulder. 'Let's start with the statue for now.'

We entered a spacious atrium with a vaulted ceiling and a three-sided cedar balcony—entirely out of character with the cramped, traditional front house. A wide sky-window offered little light, given the late hour and the overcast day.

Etta led me up yet another staircase; its wooden handrail was rough and unsteady. We moved in silence. Up top, she flipped on a weak, yellowed spotlight over a windowed cove at the house's rear. There, the object of Etta's distress stood facing away from us and towards a large picture window. I could see the back of the draped gown, cascading hair, and flowered crown, as well as a small, sculpted bird perched on the life-sized figure's left shoulder.

'This is the evil statue?' I was surprised at its beauty, especially considering the grave accusations against it.

'Come, look more closely,' Etta gestured, stepping back so I could enter the sallow sphere.

Why did she fear a thing so exquisite, with features so delicate and lifelike? Despite the stone material from which it was made, it seemed to possess a certain suppleness—as though a touch to the hair might rearrange the curling strands… or a slight breeze might flutter the gossamer gown.

But the eyes—the eyes were a different story. In contrast to the vibrancy in the face, they were blank as uncarved headstones, apart from a small, dark fissure zigzagging from just above the left brow, through the unseeing void, and down the smooth left cheek. I remembered a line I'd once read, something about *the tiny crack through which life can slip into death…*

'Don't you see?' Etta interrupted. 'The crack. It just appeared!'

'Well, old things do break sometimes.'

'But it was never here before!'

'Maybe you bumped it? Or your son?'

'I've never touched it. Not once. And Joey won't even look at it. He says it's a demon, and I believe him.'

'Well, then, let's just remove it right now, shall we?' I encircled the statue's waist, thinking I might lift it from its base. However, the entire figure had been tacked to the ground by nails, almost as if someone had wanted to ensure its position—or maybe to prevent it from leaping through the glass.

'NO!' Etta shouted. 'It's just that… well… look for yourself.'

She pointed at the dove on the figure's shoulder. There, across the bird's wings and feathers, I noticed words etched in a careful, slanted script. '*Beware the demon in the mirror*', the message read.

I was confused. Was this a threat, written on a bird's wing? What demon? And what mirror?

Suddenly, I felt claustrophobic. The smell was getting to me, as were Etta's strange stories and the whole cursed statue thing. I needed some fresh air.

'Etta, I have an appointment… I'm sorry I need to go—I'll do some investigating for you this weekend.'

I rushed down and out, aware but uncaring of my rudeness. My hands shook as I fumbled to open my car. My neck pricked; I glanced back at the house through the damp dusk just as a white shape shifted between the trees in the side yard. Had Etta followed me out? I checked the front window—and there she was, walking past the kitchen with a brown fur—probably her quilt. But there it was again: a white streak, now obscured behind the lilac bush. Was it Joey, hiding outside to spite his mother? Looking up, I saw Joey's lanky silhouette seated at his curtained window. *Must be a neighbor's dog,* I thought... until the form glided from behind the bush. I gasped as the tall, draped figure swept silently across the grass before passing straight through the house's southern wall—the only discernible trace a long, curling tendril floating behind it before all was swallowed by stone.

***

That night, a thick, choking cloud seemed to have settled about my head. I felt unable to think or focus on work. Annie and I had been exploring the 'language' of weather—the way the sky speaks to the water in exhales and inhales. In fact, the entire evaporation process is just that: a breathing apparatus, with weather nothing more than the effect of various forces on that process. I wondered about the day, about Etta's torment, and imagined it all a nuanced weather system, picking up energies and redistributing them elsewhere. The question was, what unseen force was powering the storm?

I hardly slept; the statue haunted my dreams. In one it glided through my bedroom wall and stood next to my bed. An unseen clock ticked louder and louder as the blank eyes inched closer to my face, jarring my dream-self awake. Dream-me asked the figure what she wanted. Distant windchimes tinkled; a sweet, jasmine-scented gust blew chalky dust from the figure's eyes, revealing two mirrors—a doubling of my own reflection. I studied my face in them; my image dissolved and morphed first into Etta, then a flower, then a wasp—and at last into a waterfall, my own thunderous rush jolting the real me awake just as my alarm rang. My head felt sodden and scattered, but I knew what I had to do and arranged for the morning off.

Heading down Montview Avenue towards the Denver Library, the Rocky Mountains blushed pink along the morning skyline. I arrived at the grand, white-columned building just as it opened for the day. My first stop was the *Historic City Records* collection on the seventh floor; there, among rows of cherrywood shelves, I found the landowner records for 969 Spruce Street. I also happened upon a copy of *The Urban Tattler: Firsthand Accounts from 20th Century Denver.* Settling into a red velvet chair next to a stained-glass window, I began to dig in.

Just as last October's *Post* had relayed, the city had disturbed scores of unclaimed remains, to make way for 'progress' in the Whitman Gardens neighborhood, where 969 Spruce stood. The house itself had been built by an L. S. Farley, a registered taxidermist known as 'The Skinner' by locals. *The Tattler* featured an entire page on the place: a dramatic account of the man—rumored to have killed and stuffed hundreds of animals, mostly for sport—as well as details of his implication in myriad missing animal reports. Farley's wife, Lore, and an unnamed rumored child were said to have disappeared in 1915 (Farley had claimed they'd run off, but townspeople had become increasingly wary of him). Just before his death, Farley had alerted officials that he'd been stalked and threatened by 'ghostly beasts'. In 1916, a neighbor discovered Farley's bitten and hoof-trampled body in his front yard (the death date was verified; the injuries were not).

The official deeds showed that after Farley's death, the Whitmans—whose ample estate had, by then, shrunk to its current twenty acres—had mysteriously repurchased the house at 969 Spruce. The new owner's deed named none other than Iris Whitman—a startling detail, given my 'acquaintance' with her back at the gardens. No records existed after 1920, so I planned to ask Etta whether she'd bought or rented the place.

Next, I checked the *20th Century Periodicals* collection on the library's third floor. In one of the many rows of heavy steel drawers, I had a 'Eureka!' moment; I found a public notice for 'The Denver Society Sculpture Exhibit of 1917', which featured a work by none other than Iris Whitman herself. One commentator had remarked how, given recent accusations regarding Mrs. Whitman's 'dabblings in heresy', the show's attendance might be sparse. I searched for more on this, and found a community calendar post for November 7 of the same year:

JOHN DEE SOCIETY MEETING; 969 SPRUCE STREET; TONIGHT'S TOPIC: THE SPIRIT MIRROR (to be led by Iris Whitman).

'John Dee Society'? 'Spirit mirror'? I wanted to know more but found nothing in the stacks. However, a glazed-eyed librarian with square black glasses and a peppered beard was eager to help. He clicked his keyboard in swift bursts, then printed off three pages for me.

'So John Dee talked to angels through some piece of stone, huh?' he half-asked, adjusting the thick frames on his round nose. 'I'd never heard of him—a real 16th century occultist! Think I'll have to read up on him myself, if you don't mind?'

'Have at it. And thank you!'

I left the place feeling like I'd traveled a thousand miles with no clear way back. Like the kids in *Hansel and Gretel,* I feared I'd ventured too far into the woods—however, instead of scattering crumbs, I'd left puddles.

***

I'd intended to revisit Etta the following week; however, she telephoned that afternoon, her words strident and tumbling. Joey had done something horrible; the root in the laundry room had bored through the thick wooden door and was now climbing the back stairs. My first thought was that Etta needed medical help—she sounded unwell. She begged me to come by.

I drove straight over, thinking I'd contact her landlord myself (if she had one) to take over the chaos. As I drove up, I was surprised at how ordinary the place looked in daylight. It was a typical, if undermanaged, two-story Denver bungalow—far from the sinister place I recalled from last night. The worn brick façade seemed almost charming behind the untrimmed hedges, even on this dull afternoon. Two white trucks were parked out front—one a tree service, the other branded 'Pete's Plumbing'. The front door had been left open; I entered and called out for Etta.

'Louise, come quick! Back here!'

Etta, wearing the same blue dress as the day before, was leaning dangerously over the thin wooden balcony railing. Her eyes were swimming, the pupils turbulent pools encircled in white.

'Etta? What's the matter? Be careful!' I was sure she'd tumble off the balcony any second.

'Joey murdered them!' her voice quavered.

'Murdered? Who?' I was climbing the wobbly steps; something sharp pierced my skin… a splinter.

Etta approached me, cradling a mangled bird's nest with two crushed blue eggs and a smashed baby bird. My stomach twisted—unaided by the moldy stench, which had grown even more pungent than yesterday.

'He did this, Louise. My baby is a monster!' she wailed.

I considered what to say. 'Have you talked to his doctor, maybe a child therapist?'

'A child what? Heavens, no.'

'But maybe—'

'He went away, Louise. He disappeared. He always does.'

'Sometimes kids need their space. Don't worry, Etta, he'll be back.'

She cursed the statue again, blaming it for Joey and for the snake that had slithered from the kitchen drain last night. She'd smashed it with a frying pan, because what other choice had there been?

Both the arborist and the plumber were already at work. Between the whirring chainsaw, the clanging pipes, and Etta's cries, I was in the middle of some dissonant, angst-driven symphony.

'Etta, this may be none of my business, but I wondered whether you've reported all this to your landlord? Or… are you the owner—I'm sorry to ask.'

'Oh no, he hasn't spoken to me in years. He despised my husband, you see.'

I wanted to pry further, but Etta seemed in a hurry to get to the statue.

'You must see this, Louise.'

'Of course—and then I'll share what I found at the library today.'

As we neared the figure, Etta stifled a whimper. I must admit, I was startled to see that the white face had split wide open, exposing a mass of black wasps oozing up from within the figure's mouth, like a dark secret held too long. I recalled the wasp in my dream.

Etta tore off a wooden slat from the railing. With a clenched jaw, she raised it high and charged the figure.

'It's the demon! I'll kill you!'

'Etta, stop! Look—they aren't attacking; not one is even flying. They must have built a nest in there. Maybe the arborist can capture and relocate them?'

Etta lowered the plank with a *thud*, her chest shuddering. She seemed both here and somewhere else, far away.

Nature speaks in symbols, I thought. So why wasps? I know they're inherently gentle creatures, contrary to their reputation. Unless directly provoked, they care less for aggression and more for finding food. I tried to be still, to listen for the message…

THWACK.

Etta was back swinging at the statue. A large chunk of the

rose-crowned head sailed past me and smashed through the glass window. The wasps reacted swiftly, their once-gentle buzz rising to a swelling growl.

With army-like precision, they flew through the jagged window to the arborist on his ladder. His startled face disappeared in an inky swirl, sending the saw screaming upwards, out of his hand—and then, horror of horrors, back down to knock him off his perch with an awful shriek… then a gruesome grinding… and, at last, a low, wasting murmur. Etta stood gaping, the fractured plank still raised.

'DEMON!' she howled, her face as red as her hair as she thrashed the crumbling stone again and again, finishing off the head, then the torso, and at last sending a graceful white arm wheeling off the railed edge to shatter on the floor below. I reached for my phone's emergency button, remembering the injured man outside.

BOOM! CRACK!

The house shook; the balcony buckled, and both Etta and I careened across the floor towards the wall.

'What? An earthquake?!' My phone had skidded towards the stairs.

Another sudden jolt. The floor see-sawed violently. I tried to stand, but collapsed near the statue, now a mere pile of stones and dead wasps. Within the rubble I saw something gleam—a polished, silvery something. I reached for it, but the object was lodged inside a larger fragment: the forehead and right eye. I pried it out carefully, then stuffed it into my jacket pocket just in time.

'Etta! Move! Run!'

The wasps had filed back in; the swarm's electric buzz headed straight towards Etta. She tottered to the staircase, slipping down a few steps before…

BOOM.

The room quaked again, releasing a long, anguished thrum, like the last cry of a dying animal.

SNAP.

The staircase severed from the balcony, its balusters tumbling like a child's stick house. Etta, batting her face madly in the fading light, could reach neither balcony nor ground, since the floorboards below were bursting off in fountains of rancid water.

'Hold onto the steps! I'll try to get to you!'

In the purpled shadows, I caught flashes of Etta's stunned, puffy face. She began babbling unintelligibly—something about a pistol and Joey and someone named Leroy.

I rolled to the balcony's edge and yanked off a dangling beam. Etta's lower body was now fully submerged in the fast-rising water. Wood and debris bobbed to the surface; the pallid cove light fizzled off. I held out the beam as far as was possible from my lurching ledge.

'Etta! Grab this, please—!'

She extended her arm, then fell back, the treads beneath her rocking like a capsized canoe. 'Help!' she shrieked. 'The root! The root!' She reached out again, her eyes frantic… just a few more inches…

CREAK! CRACK!

The balcony gave way just as a thick, barked tendril rose from the depths, wrapped itself around Etta's neck, and wrenched her into the roiling chaos.

'ETTA!'

I tumbled into the murky water, my chest bursting with terror. I could hear Etta's gurgling screams as I clawed through the wet darkness. The surge was violent and gushing, a shark's open jaw—and Etta and I its inevitable prey. I searched for an escape route in my mind, remembering the balcony window and its border of leafy ivy. Might there be a trellis supporting the vine? It was worth a try.

Something bobbed up near my face; I held it up in the blue-gray light and saw that it was the skull of a large mammal. And then they all rose: ten, twenty, a hundred beastly carcasses, many yet intact as though held together by invisible wire. The fear engulfed me; I coughed and choked, kicked and pushed away the bones… and above it all, the *tick, tick, tick* of the clock echoed still from the far room, as though time itself had eclipsed all sense.

At last—and by luck, given the blinding darkness, my shoe struck the wilted balcony floor. I scrambled up, my feet slipping backwards, my fingers sliding painfully down the splintered wood. I made slow progress up, and up, until there it was: the rear window, obscured now by the spiked, jutting branches of a half-cut pine. Given the curve of the wall, I later surmised that the entire back house had been leaning on the property's last remaining tree.

Grasping the ragged pane, I reached through the sharp boughs. Thankfully, the trellis was there. I scrambled to remove my jacket, wrapped it around my face, and forced my way through—my arms pricked and scratched with a thousand needles.

As I hit the ground, the entire back house seized, releasing a long, tortured groan. Sensing the danger, I dashed to the side yard just as the back wall gave way to a massive torrent that drenched the streets for half a mile.

***

Out front, flashing lights lined the block. Curious neighbors gawked; a man in a yellow hardhat shouted into his phone about a plumbing accident involving the city water main. Someone asked me if I needed medical attention, which I declined.

An elderly couple stood watching from the porch next door. Still dripping and shaken, I approached them.

'Excuse me, is Etta out here? Have you seen her?'

'Etta? Etta who?' the pink-robed woman asked.

'The lady who lived there… your neighbor?'

'Goodness, no! That house has been empty forever. Property of the Whitman Society. Do you need a towel, dear? Or a bandage for your arm? Those scratches look nasty.'

'I'm okay, thanks. But wait—you never met Etta? The woman with the teenage son?'

'You must have the wrong place,' the stocky, balding husband replied. '969 was condemned, boarded up years ago. The entire foundation's rotten, they told us… with some five hundred decomposed mammal corpses down there. Guess some guy a century ago was looney tunes, you know what I mean?'

'They did bring the bulldozers a few years back—remember, Larry?' the wife added. 'But there were toxicity issues.'

I walked off, all social graces gone.

The temperature had dropped, and most of the onlookers had gone home to check their basements. A young police officer with a friendly smile approached me for questioning. I told him everything I knew; I doubted he believed a word.

'We'll have a preliminary report in a few hours,' he said. 'You're free to go.'

Instead, I sat on the curb and watched. Officials came and went, lights flickered on and off, and the cleanup had already begun. Just before dawn, the same officer approached me again.

'Hey, shouldn't you be getting home? If your story's true, I'd say you need rest.'

'What have you found so far? I won't sleep until I know—well, anything.'

The officer glanced backwards, then adjusted his blue hat and spoke quietly.

'Okay, this is all off record, so no word to anyone, right?'

'Right.'

He confided that, among the hundreds of cadavers found in the flood, the remains of two humans—they'd guessed a woman and a teenage boy—had been recovered as well.

'Remains? As in bodies?' I gulped.

'Oh no, ma'am, these bones were at least a hundred years old. But, again, the forensic team hasn't verified anything.'

'Oh, gosh… '

'And then there was this.' He unwrapped the package under his arm; it was a gold framed photo, the one I'd seen hanging in Etta's hallway. 'Only object we found with no signs of water damage—pretty crazy, huh?'

In the image, Etta, Joey, and a sullen-looking man with a rifle posed with a well-dressed gentleman in a top hat.

'Oh my… may I see the back?'

The officer removed the yellowed picture from the glass and turned it over. '1913— Loretta Whitman Farley, Joseph Farley, Leroy "Roy" Farley, and Grandfather Charles Whitman,' the hand-scrawled inscription read.

'Need help there, miss?'

'No, thank you.'

Once in the car, I tried to piece the story together… it seemed too impossible to be true. Etta *had* been in that house; I'd seen her, I'd even *touched* her. How, then, could she have been 'Lore'—Loretta Farley—wife of the horrible 'Skinner,' and daughter of *the* Charles and Iris Whitman? How had one person existed just an hour ago, only to have lived one hundred years earlier as well?

I remembered the object in my pocket. Somehow, it had remained intact through the chaos. I held it under the cabin light, hoping for an answer. I rubbed off the white, chalky film to reveal a small, two-sided, reflective stone—likely obsidian. A 'spirit mirror'? One side had been etched with an image of the statue's face, her eyes engraved with great detail. These were the same pleading, deep-set eyes I'd seen long ago at Monet's Pond.

On the other side of the stone, I saw only my own reflection, along with lines etched in a familiar, slanted script:

The one who peers into this stone

Has demons and angels all his own.
Which one to choose? is hers to say:
To banish the dark, embrace the day.
--Iris Whitman, 1918

I finally understood the full circle—the connection between myself and Iris, the house, my work, and Nature. Iris had chosen *me*; she'd brought me to Etta, who, like Joey, had been trapped by her husband's demons—both in life and in death. Iris had understood the power of art; she'd engaged the mystical to sculpt a talisman in defiance of her family's torment… yet who would have guessed that Nature would take up arms against 969 Spruce Street—not out of revenge, but rather out of the same life-affirming sense of self-preservation shared by every other being that ever is, or was, or will be?

And so the great theme to which I've devoted my life is proven again. Everything, everywhere longs to express, to be heard. *Listen,* spoke the water at Monet Pond. *Listen,* implored the house and the mirror and the statue and even time itself. *Listen,* our demons and angels demand each day, whenever we face ourselves and our decisions.

Listen.

***

It's getting late now; even the blackbirds have headed home. Ah yes, the cigar smoke… you caught the whiff, too? Go on, then, introduce yourself. Take it from me: you never know where a long-distance friendship might lead.

After all, there are a million, billion languages just waiting to be heard and spoken. As for this one, I imagine a stately man in a tweed suit and polished black shoes. He is sending sweet, smoky signals in the language of gratitude—the most transcendent language of all. I can see him now, in the mirror of my mind, tipping his hat to you, to me, and to all who remember… for at long last, his demons have flown, and his angels have come home.

The House in Boscastle

By A J Dalton

Paul Magus knew he wasn't a bad man, not compared to quite a few men he'd known, anyway. Alright, he was no saint either, but who was? With the stresses, strains, pressures and complaints of everyday life, not to mention the rampant misinformation, no one could keep themselves entirely straight all of the time. Still, he tried to treat people fairly enough, because who knew when it might come back to bite you, otherwise? It was just prudent.

Others thought the world was dog-eat-dog, of course, but he didn't fancy either eating dogs or being eaten by dogs, so he chose not to pursue that sort of thing. At the same time, he'd never quite known what to pursue instead. He'd been searching for the answer to that a long time, until he'd realised that the search itself was his answer of sorts.

He'd spent his life as a searcher… although people were far more comfortable with him calling himself a *re*searcher. He'd researched the length and breadth of the UK, poring over dusty tomes in museum archives, abandoned churches and empty libraries, studying inscriptions in chapels, on gravestones and in mausoleums, acquiring old grimoires and parchments from antiquaries, rare book collectors and some fairly dubious 'procurers of select items', and scratching his head over obscure ritualistic drawings, the geometries of masonic architecture and the curious sigils, glyphs and seals that could often be found upon ancient door lintels, thresholds and building facades. Along the way, he'd published several books that had sold surprisingly well, *The Lost Ways and Magicks of the UK* in particular, enough for him to continue his search at least.

From time to time, the itinerant search would get lonely, for he never got to stay in one place long enough to have anything like a serious relationship. He'd missed out on starting any sort of family of his own, but – at 34 – he told himself there was still plenty of time. And he hadn't entirely missed out on company either. There'd been dalliances along the way, including numerous one-night-stands, mainly with women, the odd guy and even a married couple. Then there'd been weeks, or months even, of more regular company. In particular, he remembered a girl he'd met in Edinburgh. Abi? Hadn't that been her name? She'd had the greenest eyes, and dimples when she'd smiled. She'd begged him to stay, and he'd asked her to wait for him. He wasn't even sure he had her number anymore. He hoped she was happy, anyway.

He knew some would think him a fool. And there were moments when he thought the same. But just when he'd be tempted to give up, the search would reveal something new, like a clue, a sign or a missing piece of the puzzle. He was getting closer. He could *feel* it. He was about to solve some great mystery, catch that which eluded all humankind, uncover a powerful secret, or discover the key that unlocked… well, *everything*.

Never before had he felt as close as he did now, for the search had finally led him to the remote coastal village of Boscastle down in ancient Cornwall. Its houses and hovels were built into the black rock of a steep gorge down to the sea. The route was so twisty, turny and roundabout that you would be sure, at moments, it was taking you back up and out, as if there was a spell on the place to keep strangers out. The road, such as it was, was forced to span a cascading river over and over, bridges that would be toppled or be washed away every other year. A forlorn chapel stood on a promontory above, but it could no longer be accessed because of a land collapse, meaning it had fallen into decline and welcomed only nesting seabirds.

Having left his vehicle at the designated car park higher up, the journey down into Boscastle had led Paul from one shadowed, sea-slick path to another. Cave entrances had yawned off to one side, stony gullets to swallow the unwary, while vertiginous drops and perilous screes had presented themselves on the other. He'd had intermittent views of longer stretches of the defile, but the constant back and forth around stubborn outcroppings and bizarre natural towers meant very little was truly revealed. And the wind that came howling up from below bore a salty tang of the sea, making his eyes sting and stream, and his vision constantly blur.

He'd refused to be deterred and pressed on, going deeper and further into the harrowing and wuthering crevasse, until he was convinced he would find himself amongst the very bones of the earth itself. Yet at last the way levelled out and, rounding a pronounced shoulder of midnight rock, he stepped down into the shelter and sudden stillness of a natural harbour, low granite buildings and whitewashed stone houses huddled to either side, and the sea set beyond two giant and interlocking rocky spurs.

It was this natural harbour – one of the largest in Cornwall's dramatic coastline – that meant there'd been a fishing community here since long before recorded history, since humankind had first devised how to build boats, since the true beginning even. There had been a fishing community here many thousands of years before the arrival of Christianity.

Indeed, Christianity had never really taken here, so long, rich and powerful were the pagan culture, memory and legacy. And Paul Magus had learnt that Boscastle still had its pre-Christian tradition of wise women... actual living, breathing witches! As long as Boscastle had existed, so had its sea-witches, whose knotted and bespelled ropes had tied the wind to the sails of its fishing boats for countless generations.

He had never imagined that 'witches' were anything more than innocent women falsely accused of consorting with demons and familiars by a patriarchal Church, or a paranoid and tyrannical King James I. To learn that witches were *real*... well, it changed everything. It meant that there were once-forbidden lore and learning that might still be found. It meant there were *real* magicks to be marshalled. It meant that his search had at last brought him to that great mystery, secret or key he had always felt and intuitively known was out there. *At last!* The years of pursuit, endeavour and sacrifice had been worth it. He was not a deluded fool, a weak-minded believer, a suggestible daydreamer or a superstitious crackpot. Finally. And it was said that there was even a lone surviving speaker of Cornish in Boscastle, one of the world's earliest languages, a language that could surely give him even more.

He didn't spend any time looking for a hotel. Instead, he headed straight for the Museum of Witchcraft and Magic, reported to be at the far end of the harbour. Apparently, it was a 'living' museum, a community learning centre, with a library of arcane texts – a *librarium maleficus*. He was determined to secure some sort of privileged access, and had brought signed copies of his own works that he would generously gift to the library in return. If that didn't work, well, then he'd just have to think of some less civilized approach or tactic.

He pulled up short on the flint-slippery harbour-path. He'd stepped into the cold shadow of a stag-headed figure set above him on a wall-like crag. It was woven of wicker branches and thorns as a life-size rendition of Herne the Hunter, the

Green Man or the devil himself, possibly the avatar Baal, once worshipped as a god of weather and sailors. It was seated in almost a lotus position, with a green glass orb held in its lap by one hand and the other hand raised with two bent fingers to bestow some benefaction… or curse. The head, with glassy eyes, was lifted away from him, forked antlers seeming to impale the clouds. He couldn't quite meet its gaze from his lower elevation, which was disconcerting and frustrating, but perhaps also just as well.

He gave an involuntary shudder. 'Here as guardian or warning, I suppose,' he murmured, instinctively ducking his head as he stepped past. Should he make some offering? It was always better to be safe than sorry… but he simply didn't have any vestal virgins or sheep immediately to hand that he might sacrifice. There was never one around when you needed one.

His impish thoughts left him as he moved clear and raised his head to stare stupidly at a small house right before him, painted into the rock itself. A discreet sign declared it to be the Museum. How come he hadn't noticed it on his initial approach? He shook his head. He needed to stop being so distracted. He could have walked straight past and into the sea otherwise.

Stepping inside the door, he found himself in a low, narrow corridor that turned and disappeared at quite some distance away. He realised the dwelling was far bigger on the inside than the outside. He went forward, his tread echoing along the empty passage.

At his ear, far too close, came a voice: 'Excuse me!'

He jumped in terror. His legs all but went out from under him and he had to catch himself against the wall. He stared in bewilderment at a small alcove back where he'd entered. How had he not spotted it?

'One for the museum, is it?' asked a grey-haired but fresh-faced woman from within.

'I didn't… Yes! Sorry.'

'That's alright, my dear,' she chortled, map-like creases appearing. 'Happens quite often.' She had the hazel-orange eyes of a cat.

'I… actually, was hoping to consult your library archive. My… my name is Paul Magus.'

She clapped her hands in delight. '*The* Paul Magus?'

'You-you've heard of me?' he asked in consternation, wondering if she was playing with him.

'But of course! You're quite the celebrity amongst those who *know*.' She winked at him. 'We wondered when you'd visit us. We've almost been expecting you.'

'You-you have?'

'This way, this way!' She jumped down from the high stool on which she'd been perched and scurried off ahead of him.

He hurried after her, not wanting to lose his guide, as she took him through one dim chamber after another, up crooked staircases, past overbright and buzzing display cabinets lining walk-throughs, down ladder-like rungs, and through musty cellars of paraphernalia. Within that maze, he caught tantalising glimpses of magical dirks and wands, he negotiated his way past waxworks of sorcerers and enchanters conjuring upon patterned floors, and his head swung one way to take in a cabinet of brown, grinning skulls, some animal and some human, a shrunken head and jars of shrivelled oddities, then tilted the other way to acknowledge the usual fertility objects, and to consider a plethora of idols, effigies and gurning gargoyles. Curling photos of hammy ritual practice festooned corners, and printed information on the ancestral lines and lives of practitioners was presented behind spotlighted glass. There was a wealth of curated artefacts he would need to go through if her got the chance, to sort the sensationalist items for tourists from the genuine objects of power.

But then he was in the library and staring at shelves of leather-clad volumes, scroll-tubes and portfolios. One bookcase had every precious tome attached by a long chain, so that there was no chance of the priceless contents going astray. 'Over here is our modern collection, where we have some of your own titles, Mr Magus,' the old woman was saying. 'These are collected from around Cornwall, but only a few centuries old, so mainly in English. These are all in Old English. Do you know Old English? And these in the cabinet are thought to be from only Boscastle and the immediate environs. Some are in Cornish, so might be of little use to you, see? We usually keep them under lock and key, but since it's you… I'll let you in.' He hardly heard her. His hands were already fluttering over the spines of books, touch-reading their titles and daring to ease several out, then to place them on a nearby desk. 'I'll not keep you from your studies, then, Mr Magus. I'll check in on you from time to time. It genuinely pleases us to have you here at last. We knew you'd find your way here eventually, that you wouldn't be able to resist.'

He set to, like a man possessed. He had at last made it to the threshold of what the Masons called The Great Temple, or The Lost Temple. He'd always suspected that it was not a literal building; rather, it was that place of secret and forbidden knowledge that was to be accessed through these writings. He had come as a devotee or humble pilgrim, and through much perseverance and hardship found the means by which to enter into that sacred space, a space that could only see him utterly changed. He would hardly recognise who he'd been before. He would transcend or be transmuted into an entirely different being. At last! No more would his existence be that grey prison that he'd endured since, well, forever.

Many would not have known where to start when presented with such a wealth of information. Most would not even have known what they were looking for, given that they hadn't yet discovered it. But Paul Magus hadn't come this far not to know what he was about. He started with the Old English books, which were a mix of Church parish records, with lists of the main family names, lines and groups, and legal records, with details of religious crimes and the families which were perennial offenders. He wrote page after page of notes, tracking the Angwins, Carews, Enyses and Hockings back through the centuries, all the way to some sort of medieval census, when Boscastle had apparently been dominated by the 'Kenning' family. Surely that name was no coincidence. He was close. He could smell it, and taste it. In his mind's eye, he saw the simple but hardy stone-built structures of the village of that era, and he felt the village had been little different for many centuries preceding. He wrote with furious intensity with one hand, not even needing to look at the words his pen put down, while turning the pages of texts with the other. Was this notebook finished already? He grabbed another.

Now he moved to the texts gathered from around Cornwall, but, as he'd expected, they offered little beyond diaries of gossip, the scores of song, music and rhyme, old recipes and folktales, the occasional liturgical sermon, and personal letters and effects. One name came up more than once, however: Derwa Kenning. The putative dates for the various name-entries were centuries apart. Surely it wasn't the same person. The name must have been passed from mother to daughter. Surely.

Now he had a name, he went to the Old English legal records again. Yes. Here it was. *Derwa Kenning of Boscastle was summond for trialle for all mannere of unnaturale consorte and devilree. Alle witnesse summond attestd her goodeness and she was bothe released and pardond for the hex usery of the signe ΛV*. He made a copy in his notes.

Finally he turned to the collection from Boscastle. Many of the scrolls were brittle and creaked in protest as he tried to open them, threatening to collapse entirely – much as he hated to do it, he was forced to put them aside. There were flat and only slightly tattered pieces of parchment, however, marked with a scratchy dry-blood ink. Were these words? Was it an old dialect of Cornish? He'd had the foresight to bring several language books with him, and he set about trying to translate or decipher what he'd found.

As he peered closely at the parchment, his vision began to swim. He closed his eyes for a moment and rubbed tiredly at his brow. How long had he been at it now? He opened his eyes once more and realised just how dim the light had become. The one small window that the cell-like room allowed told him it was nearly night already. He levered himself up from the desk, and winced at the shooting pains in his legs. *Argh.* He'd pulled a muscle in his back from sitting bent forward for too long. Taking a few paces, he flicked the light switch at the wall and groaned as neon light blinded him. The buzz and flicker threatened to start a headache.

He stumbled back to the table, catching himself just in time. The parchment was directly in front of him again, its spidery signs twitching and skittering. There, in the bottom left corner of one of the pages, was her mark: *ΛV*. He couldn't help himself. Light-headed and fatigued as he was, and despite a gnawing gut – when had he last eaten? – he slid back into the chair.

It was script, he was sure of it now. Was this wynde? The wind? Or to wind? Did they all but mean the same to the sea-witches of Boscastle? This was water… big water… ah, the *sea*. And… the vessel… boat? Left… under… right… and over. He felt his heart beat faster. It was a spell or incantation. He was sure of it. It allowed the practitioner, the *witch*, the *magician*, to control the wind itself. Imagine what could be done with such power. Friendly boats could be sped faster to their destinations… enemy boats, if not fleets, could be sunk. Airplanes could be thrown down out of the sky. Crops and buildings could be levelled. Could one be carried on the wind? Would he be able to *fly* by the power of such magic? And the wind could push clouds away or bring them close, to create devastating storms or otherwise, to command the weather and the very elements themselves! He could see it as he stared into the words. He felt the rush of it. All he needed to do now was… what? Make some winding knot, to then undo it? And speak these words, his own breath a whispering wind that would grow and grow until it was the deafening roar of his will and intent? He was giddy with it, yet – suddenly – he was just as fearful that he would get the pronunciation wrong, for words of power were not to be casually spoken, in case an error turned the magic back on the speaker. If only he knew Cornish better. He had to find the speaker in Boscastle!

The air in the room stirred and the parchments shifted, then fluttered, as if about to be snatched away from him. He made a grab for them just as he became aware that the draft had been caused by a door opening somewhere behind him… and that someone had come stealing up on him while he was distracted. And they were right here now, right on top of him!

He let out a yell as he snatched and swivelled despairingly. 'No! Please! Ackk!'

'Oh, my goodness, Mr Magus! Are you quite alright?'

He stared into the uncanny orange-hazel eyes of… what was her name?

She arched an eyebrow and purred at him, 'Cat got your tongue? What do you have there? Careful.'

'I-I…' He was trapped by her gaze. 'I need to find the speaker.'

'You mean Derwa.'

He went cold. It couldn't be. 'D-Derwa Kenning?'

'That's right.'

He gulped. The witch couldn't still be living?! What… how… No. It had to be a traditional family name handed down from mother to daughter, from grandmother, to… great-grandmother… down through untold generations. But something in his gut, in his water, in his very bones actually, told him it was more than a name simply being handed down. His scalp itched and the back of his neck prickled. In a quiet voice – which, even so, was too loud for the room – he confirmed, 'I *need* to see her.'

'The mistress doesn't have much time for visitors, I'm afraid, Mr Magus. People invariably attempt to see her because they *want* something from her. She finds it… rude. It's demanding, presumptuous and disrespectful, you see. She asks me to keep people away, to guard her, as it were. Or to make it clear that there will be some price to pay if she agrees to any sort of visit.'

He backed away, and she stalked silently after him, a playful smile on her lips. He was in no doubt that the creature before him was some sort of familiar. His mind was screaming, but all he could manage was a wheeze: 'Wh-what sort of price?'

'Weeell, now.' He caught a glimpse of sharp incisors. 'Even the answer to such a question comes at a price. Why should knowledge be freely given away, especially when, as they say, knowledge is power or too much knowledge can be *dangerous*? Hmm?'

'I'll pay it!'

'Careful, Mr Magus.'

'I will pay.' And he found he meant it. He hadn't come so far and sacrificed so much to give up now, to return to a meek or humdrum life all the while knowing that a greater existence had been within his grasp and his for the taking if he'd but had the courage for it.

She tutted. 'Even if it should be some terrible price, Mr Magus? Are you truly willing? I will ask one last and final time, advising you that this will be the bargain sealed and done.'

'I will pay the price… w-whatever it is.'

Her eyes gleamed, and she grinned as she made the pronouncement: 'Then it is a compact now and forever. So be it. Please, replace the parchments, for you will have no need of them. Follow me, and I will conduct you into the presence of the mistress. We will be able to find our way easily enough, for it is a full moon tonight. This way, Mr Magus.'

***

The familiar led him back out of the museum's maze. As they passed the effigy of Baal in the moonlight, Paul felt a chill run through him, as if to his very soul. He dared not look up, for fear that – this time – the devil's gaze would be there looking right into him. Instinctively, he went to cross himself, but found he did not have the strength to do it.

The angry roar of the distant sea was all he heard, and tremors came up through his feet, putting him on edge and hurting his very teeth, as waves attacked and pounded the rock beyond the harbour. There was no one to be seen, as if the village had been abandoned. And he saw that every window was shuttered so tightly that not even light escaped from within the fishing cottages – there was no sign of life to attract whatever might prowl the alleys of Boscastle once the sun had gone down.

What have I done?

'Here we are, Mr Magus.'

He blinked. They stood before a heavy and low building that looked to have been carved from the very bedrock so as to withstand the withering elements that had beset the village across all time. There were no windows or shutters to be seen, just a short iron-banded door set deep into an external wall that had to be several feet thick. There were neither a doorhandle nor keyhole in evidence.

'H-how is it I did not notice this house when I first arrived?' he dared.

The familiar shook her head. 'I think you already know the answer to that, Mr Magus. Besides, people only see what they expect or want to see most of the time. You must choose your door, Mr Magus. The mistress will know you are here.'

'I… umm… sorry?'

'Walk around the house. Choose your door, or perhaps a door will choose you. No. *Anti*-clockwise, Mr Magus. That's it. Go along.'

As instructed, her went round the corner of the building to

his right. The wall was all but the same as the one before, except the door set into it seemed to be made of a natural clouded glass. He tentatively reached out and touched it, yelping and hastily withdrawing his hand. The surface was colder than anything he'd ever known. He continued on round the building. The next door was woven of what looked like living brambles, with a good number of leaves in evidence. He cried out as thorns pricked the ends of his fingers. He sucked on them and tasted blood… and… he prayed to all that was holy and unholy that he wasn't now poisoned. The final door was a mirrored surface, but the image he saw there had him sobbing and fleeing in horror. *What has become of me?*

And he ran back to the first door. The familiar was gone… but the door! It was ajar. He crept up to it, then reared back at the intensity of the heat coming from within. It had to be a test. If the speaker was within then, no matter the inferno inside, it had to be survivable. And she wouldn't wait forever, he knew. If he was going to cross the threshold, it had to be now.

He moved quickly – before his courage could fail him – pushing the door wide enough to step inside, and then using his back to close it behind him. He gagged with the ferocity of the hissing, raging blaze in the hearth on the other side of the shadowy room. He felt his lungs shrivelling and his forehead and face were already slick with sweat – his eyes stung and swam. She was there in a chair between the light and the dark – the air was shimmering. Her back was to him. Did she gesture towards the other seat?

He was so terrified he did not have the wit to think anymore. He went to the chair and sat. He felt his eyelashes and eyebrows crisp. He turned away from the fire and she caught him in her glare. The moisture left his eyes and all he saw now was blood-tinged.

'Mistress,' he croaked.

Words, like beauty, were irrelevant. He was in her thrall.

She was. That was all and everything. She defined him entirely.

She spoke the words of power he had so long craved.

Then she stated her price: 'Your youth and years, so that I may continue.'

He staggered out of the house in Boscastle, a geriatric. His strength was barely sufficient to keep upright. The knowledge and power he now possessed kept the elements back from him, then bent them so that they supported him up.

He determined to find a place where he might write down all that had occurred, as a warning to others. He hoped he would manage to put it all down before his last gasp.

End.

Upon Reflection

By J.McDonald

The shock of the cold water locks my lungs and makes it impossible to catch my breath. My head isn't under — but it's just as hard to breathe as if it was. I thrash about, desperate to ease the vice-like grasp around my ribcage. There's only icy steel blue visible in every direction. I can feel the pressure of the lifejacket under my armpits and I'm grateful I have it on.

Something's not right, though. As I struggle to get a grip on what's happened, something nags at me — like an insistent child poking you until you pay attention to them.

***

My eyes are suddenly wide and I'm doubled up, my muscles paralysed — locking me into a fetal position — as I lay in bed drenched in a cold sweat. I slowly take in my surroundings. My body tries to relax but my mind can't. I lay there gasping, trying to focus on anything except the visions that have haunted my sleep for the past ten years. At last, I manage to reach for the bottle next to my bed and take a clumsy swig. The gentle burn of my self-prescribed remedy heats my inner core and helps to dull the remnants of the nightmare. Finally finding some relief, with a groan, I stretch for my phone to check the time.

'Late again,' I sigh exhaustedly, flopping back onto my pillow — my hand still gripping the bottle. 'Time to face the day.' I take another quick gulp of warmth to prepare me for going out into such a cold world.

***

Closing the door behind me, I slide on my aviators. The sun is bright and the dull ache of my head makes darkness preferable. The trip to the nursing home won't take long but, because of the time, I grab a cab instead of walking. A woman with a rowdy child clutched tightly in each hand gives me a dirty look as I slide into the back seat of the ride she'd had her eye on.

'You snooze, you lose,' I laugh under my breath. *Her inability to use birth control isn't my problem.*

We pull up in front of the home and the cabbie mutters something as I get out of the car — probably a colourful opinion on my lack of a tip.

'When someone starts tipping me for doing my job, then I'll start tipping everyone else for doing theirs,' I say to no one in particular.

The Seniors' Retirement Complex I've arrived at reminds me more of an asylum from a horror movie than the luxurious reward for a life of hard work that the billboard out front tries to sell you.

I can't believe they'd rather have her rot away in here than let me take care of her. It pisses me off, thinking about what I could do with that money — the better care she would get. *Even if they don't trust me to look after her, the least they could do is fork out the cash for a better place than this — it's not like they can't afford it.*

I need to calm down before I go in. I decide to have a quick smoke and distract myself with some people-watching. A couple of orderlies who look like they're on break are hanging out near the corner of the building. Leaning against the wall, I listen in on their conversation to pass the time. A squat little man with a buzz cut is talking.

'They can't help themselves. I don't know if they're just getting dumber or if it's because they're intrinsically drawn to self-destruction. I don't even have to bait the traps anymore — they just seem to wander in all on their own.'

Gross, I think to myself. *I knew this place was bad, but I didn't think it was lousy enough to have a rat problem. I guess I shouldn't be surprised though.*

A taller, almost cadaverous man replies: 'Well, of course they do — they're vermin. They don't know any better.'

'Want to make a wager on how many I can catch in the next month? You can set the terms for types of trap.'

Because sadistic bets about how many creatures someone can torture isn't my idea of fun, I decide it's finally time to head in. The interior of the home isn't much better than the exterior. The air reeks of stale potpourri and old people. The dingy yellow wallpaper always reminds me of that Charlotte Perkins Gillman story. It makes me itch to key the walls — like you would some douchebag's car.

Gran's room isn't as bad. I'd painted it a pale green for her when she moved in. She has a large window that overlooks the garden out back and my parents found it in their hearts to shell out enough dough to get her a private room. The space is small, with only a bed, night table, dresser, and armchair. I usually steal the plastic seat next to the elevator whenever I come to visit. Most of the old folks have walkers they can sit on while they wait so I don't feel too guilty about borrowing it. Gran is in bed today so I luck out and get to sit in the comfy armchair instead.

'Hey Gran, how's it going?'

A big smile spreads across her wrinkled crepe paper face.

'Jordan, good morning… or should I say afternoon? You're late,' she says with a little wink. 'Come here and give me a hug.'

Having given her an affectionate squeeze, I take a seat in the armchair. We go through our routine pleasantries and small talk which has begun to feel like a ritual — words that are uttered automatically, ceremonially.

Not long into my visit, one of the orderlies I'd seen outside pokes his head into the room to let Gran know it's almost tea time. It's the shorter man, who now reminds me slightly of a vulture. His neck and head are stooped forward, his shoulders slightly raised, and his eyes… his eyes look as though they're scanning, hunting for a carcass to feed on. I can picture him pocketing jewellery and loose change as he moves about the rooms of all those who've been put here to suffer through the remainder of their existence.

This has *me* scanning the room to see what he might plan to nip from my grandmother. I quickly spot a gold pocket watch she has sitting on her night table. Immediately, I flick my gaze back to the orderly and, sure enough, he's been staring in the exact same direction.

I'll have to take that with me to keep it safe. I can tell Gran that I'm getting it polished or something.

As soon as the orderly leaves the room, I quietly slide the watch into my pocket. My grandmother is rummaging through her dresser looking for a sweater. I haven't been paying close attention to their conversation so I'm a little lost when she says, 'Oh, that Sammy is such a kidder. You know he's always in here trying to get me to live a little, break some rules.'

'Sounds like a rascal. What kind of rules is he trying to get you to break?'

'He's not fussy about that, just as long as it's something fun. He says a little trouble would make me feel young again but I've told him that I'm perfectly content with being old. I'll leave the trouble up to you kids,' she laughs, as she pinches my cheek.

I ignore my grandmother's comment and help her down to

the dining room for tea.

***

The icy water has seized my muscles, making it next to impossible to move. But I have to move. I have to find something… something I've lost. I try to kick my feet, to keep moving, to feebly push aside the water with hands burning from the cold. It's not here, whatever it is. That means… it must be sinking.

'No!'

My own shouting wakes me from the nightmare. Falling asleep on the couch is never a good idea. My neck and lower back feel like someone's had me in a torture device all night. Between the pain, and the memories that need to be shaken off, I decide it's time for more medicine.

After rolling a joint, I reach into my pocket for my lighter. My fingers find both the familiar light-weight plastic of a cheap Bic and an unfamiliar heavy metal disc. Pulling both from my pocket, I suddenly remember grabbing my Gran's pocket watch.

After lighting up, I rub my thumb across the smooth back of the watch and notice how warm it is. I flip it over and the front is covered in an intricate pattern that surrounds some lettering at the centre — the words aren't in a language I recognize though. Clicking the release, the watch pops open.

Inside, on the right, is a fairly ordinary-looking clock face and, on the left, is a mirror. I catch a glimpse of myself in it and quickly close the watch again. It appears I'm in need of a shower and a good night's sleep. Half-heartedly, I decide to take care of one of those things — the one that's not likely to result in more nightmares.

My shower has made me late for work so I throw on some clothes and head out the door. Driving would get me there faster than taking the bus so it seems like a good time to ask for a favour. Luckily, my neighbour is usually pretty generous with the old mini-van parked out front. I knock on the door and try my best to look charmed by whatever lame attempts at flirting are about to come my way as the door swings open.

'Hey, Ash. I was wondering if I could borrow the van. I wanted to go pick up some things for my Gran after work and it'd be easier if I didn't have to take the bus.'

Ash leans against the door frame and takes a minute to appreciate the view.

'Well sure, Jordan, anytime. And if you ever need a hand with your errands, or *anything* else, you just let me know.'

This not-so-subtle offer is followed with a wink as the keys are tossed to me.

'Oh, I will, don't you worry,' I say with a grin that I hope doesn't betray just how repulsive that idea is.

I spin around quickly to leave and accidentally bash my hip on the wall. Something hard in my pocket makes the impact feel like it's sure to leave a bruise. When I get to the van, I check to see what it was and find my grandmother's watch. *Funny, I don't remember grabbing it.* I quickly pop it open to check to see if I've done any damage.

The clock is okay but there's a hairline crack running across the mirror and something weird in the reflection. I try rubbing it with my shirt but the smudge, or whatever it is, won't come off. I bring it closer to get a better look. The mark isn't on the surface, but underneath. As I stare at it, the spec grows larger and turns red, twisting into a long thick blob. The slug-like shape shifts and squirms then splits partway down the middle taking on the appearance of a forked tongue.

My heart is pounding and I nearly jump out of my skin when someone knocks at the window. I clench my fist, snapping the watch shut.

'Having trouble getting it started?' Ash asks with that same all-too-friendly smile.

It takes a minute for my head to clear. I jam the key in

the ignition, smile back, then quickly pull out into the road. Catching the time on the dashboard, I'm reminded of just how late I am and realize I may need to break a few traffic laws if I'm going to keep my job — my hallucination quickly forgotten.

***

When I get to work, Ronnie is standing at the door, over-dramatically pointing to the clock on the wall.

'The only reason you even still have a job is you're the best at sniffing out how to talk people into taking a bigger loan than they come in here for.'

I know I'm on thin ice, so I try to scrape together an excuse. 'Sorry, Ronnie. There was a bad accident and the road was closed. I had to take a huge detour.'

'It's always something with you. From now on, you arrive on time or you lose your shift. Go clean out the coffee maker and put on a fresh pot.'

I attempt to keep the loathing I feel for Ronnie out of my expression as I make my way to the back. 'Someone's on a power trip this morning,' I mutter under my breath.

After scrubbing what's left of the gelatinous goo out of the bottom of the pot, I start a fresh batch, when inspiration suddenly strikes. *I think I'll do them all a favour and add a little "flavour shot".* I take a quick look around to make sure I'm alone, then add one last ingredient to the pot. It will be like a low-stakes game of Russian roulette to see who gets it. Honestly, I don't really care who it is.

***

Somehow, I survive the day and escape the building as quickly as possible when it's over. I'm not ready to face the tedium that is my apartment — or the clumsy advances that await when I return the van — so I drive around aimlessly for a while. I eventually happen upon a crowded park. Eavesdropping is usually better than anything on TV, so I pick a bench and settle in.

Not only does this turn out to be somewhat entertaining, but it also happens to turn a profit. After listening to some poor sap trying to convince his girlfriend not to break up with him for about thirty minutes, a couple of kids run by me on their way to the concession stand. In all her excitement for a treat, one little tyke forgets to keep a firm grasp of her money. Her loss is my gain and, to reward myself for helping our youth learn a valuable lesson, I decide to treat myself to something a little more grownup than what she would've been planning to buy.

***

Later that evening, after I've had enough alcohol to help me drown out some of my day, I lazily remember my grandmother's watch, the incident from earlier chemically blurred in my memory. Reaching into my pocket, I'm struck again by how warm it is. If I hadn't known better, I'd think there was a slow-burning heat source inside of it. Idly, I open the clasp.

'Shit.'

Somehow, the crack from earlier has gotten worse. Now there's a spiderweb of fissures winding across the mirrored side. I rub my thumb across its surface to check if any of the pieces are loose. That's when I see it again — that sinister forked tongue. The image is distorted by the fractures that have formed in the glass. I blink to try and clear my vision, but there seems to be more to it than I'd noticed before.

Above the tongue there appears to be a set of hideous fangs that drip with a venomous yellow substance. In another section, I catch a glimpse of a stunted bat-like nose. Above it is a pair of beady black eyes, constantly rolling and looking off in a new direction, never settling into a steady gaze. In one of the larger chunks, a tall hairy ear — like that of a donkey — is visible. And in yet another, a pair of grubby raccoon-like paws are greedily rubbing themselves together.

I toss the watch on the coffee table and cover my face with my hands in an attempt to block the pictures from my mind. A wave of nausea sends bile bubbling up my throat. *What the hell is wrong with me? It's just a hallucination.*

Paranoid, I look over my shoulder. Part of me hopes to see an explanation for the reflection, while part of me fears to see the grotesque parts forming some hideous whole. *Am I simply losing it?*

'I've just gotta get more sleep,' I try convincing myself.

Slightly comforted by this logic, I figure the only way to feel better is to follow my own advice. After popping some pills, to make me oblivious to the rest of the world for a while, I flop onto my bed.

***

The water is unbearably cold, but I have to dive under. The lifejacket makes this impossible. My fingers, which are somehow simultaneously numb and on fire, claw at the zipper that's helping to keep me afloat. I can't make them work. I struggle to tilt my head down so that I can see what I'm doing and, there, where my hands should be, are a set of lanky fur-covered claws.

Instantly, I'm wide awake and looking frantically about the room. I don't know what I'm looking for until my eyes land on the watch still laying where I'd tossed it the night before. The nightmare has me more shaken than usual. A manic anxiety to be anywhere but here overcomes me.

I don't know what time it is and, frankly, I don't care.

Quickly throwing on some clothes, I grab the watch, and the van keys I'd failed to return the day before. I feel hunted — like I need to be moving to stay alive.

I drive around for several hours with no particular destination in mind. I make turns and change direction at random so often that it takes me a while to figure out where I am when I eventually calm down.

'You've gotta get a grip, Jordan, they're just dreams.' This would be reassuring if I knew that I could trust myself, but visions of the creature in the watch have now added to the list of things haunting me, and I'm growing less certain of my own sanity.

So ditch the watch and have one less thing to worry about. Who cares if that orderly ends up stealing it?

'Yeah, it's not even mine. I'll just take it back to Gran and be done with it.'

Somewhat relieved to have a plan, I make my way over to the nursing home. When I get up to my grandmother's room her face lights up with a huge smile.

'Jordan, I didn't expect to see you again so soon.'

'Hey, Gran. I wanted to return this. I borrowed your watch and thought it was time to bring it back.'

When I remove the watch from my pocket her face falls a little. She automatically stretches out her hand for it and I feel relieved the second it slips from my fingers into hers. Immediately, she opens the casing and looks inside. I hadn't considered what would happen if she opened it. I wince, knowing that the mirror is in worse condition than when I took it. I'd been so distracted by what I'd seen beneath the surface, that I'd completely forgotten about the broken glass. *At least she won't see the monster hiding in there — she's not crazy.*

'Oh, Jordan,' she says in a whisper, 'there're so many cracks.'

'I'm sorry about that, Gran. I dropped the watch and meant to get it repaired before I brought it back.'

She seems oblivious to what I've said. 'How long have you

had this?' she asks in an quiet voice.

'Just the one day.'

I'm not entirely sure what this has to do with anything but my answer seems to stab her like a knife. Tears begin rolling down her cheek as I come to sit beside her on the bed. She reaches up to place her hand on my shoulder and looks straight into my eyes.

'One day? All of these cracks are from one day?'

I don't understand her fixation with the amount of time it took me to break her watch. I reach for it, feeling ashamed. 'I'll go take it to get fixed right now.'

She quickly jerks back her hand, keeping the watch out of my reach. 'You weren't meant to have this yet, Jordan. I would have explained it all to you when it was time for you to have it.'

What could there possibly be to explain about a watch? I know how to tell time. 'I don't understand what you mean. If you'll let me have it, I can take it to someone to fix.'

'You're the only one who can fix this, Jordan. No one else can do it for you.' When I don't say anything, she continues: 'People used to believe that mirrors could show you your soul. That's why breaking one is supposed to be bad luck — but luck has nothing to do with these cracks.'

I don't know what she's talking about and I'm starting to get concerned that her brain's a little addled. Her gaze has moved back to stare at the damage and she continues to speak, almost as if she's in a trance.

'This is a special watch, Jordan — more of a compass really. Did you see the inscription on the outside?' She doesn't wait for my reply but continues in a hushed tone. 'It means "Time is precious, use it wisely." Oh, Jordan, how have you been spending your time?' And with that, she begins to sob.

'Gran, I don't understand.' I place my hand on her back but she doesn't react at all: she just keeps weeping.

When her tears finally begin to subside, she looks up at my face. Her gaze seems to search my features, looking for

I-don't-know-what.

Just then, Sammy pokes his pinched, beaky face in through the door. 'Time for your physio, Maia.'

Gran quickly wipes her eyes and waves him off without turning around. 'I'm busy right now, Sammy. I'll go tomorrow instead.' She takes a deep breath to settle herself.

'No can do, Maia. The schedule is fully booked and the doctor says you need to follow your routine as prescribed.'

'One day isn't going to make any difference,' she says stubbornly.

'Sorry, my dear. I'm not going to take no for an answer. I'll wait outside until you've said goodbye.' Sammy gives me a wink as he closes the door.

Defeated, Gran sighs. 'Come back tomorrow, Jordan, and I'll try to explain things more.'

Because I can see how exhausted she is, I simply nod my head, then help her stand up. As we make our way to her door, Gran gestures back towards the bed.

'Jordan, you forgot the watch. You have to take it with you. It's yours now.'

Her weary and forlorn tone, combined with her outburst of earlier, has me speechless and confused. I snatch the watch from where it lies then finish helping her into Sammy's waiting arms. I avoid anymore eye contact with either of them and, as soon as I've handed her over, decide to take the stairs so that I don't have to spend the elevator ride down with them.

What the hell was that all about? I need to clear my head — or at least try to erase the memory of Gran's sadness. I head to the closest bar and begin blurring the image of her devastated face the best way I know how.

After a few hours, I've sufficiently numbed myself and decide to head back to my apartment to catch up on some sleep. The bartender offers to call me a cab but I lie and say I'm going to walk.

***

For the first time in years, I awake from a dreamless sleep. It's dark — I can't see anything — but I can hear a slow drip, drip, drip in the distance. Then it starts to come back to me: the blurry headlights, my overcompensation to avoid them, the minivan tumbling like clothes in a dryer — somehow soft, gentle, and slow.

Shit. That dripping is probably leaking gas. I don't smell any fuel but I struggle to sit up and am suddenly aware that I can't move at all. Panic begins to set in. *No, this can't be happening. Not again!* Only this time it doesn't seem to be the bitter cold that has me frozen in place.

I'm momentarily grateful for the fact that, unlike last time, I was alone when I set out tonight. With this realization, all of the memories come flooding back and there's no drugs or drinks within reach to stop them. With the memories comes the inescapable truth that I have no one to blame but myself. After all, this is as much my own fault as it was when he drowned that day.

We were young and, when you're young, you think you know everything — you think that you're invincible. He'd trusted me. He'd trusted me to take care of him, to protect him. For years I've blamed him for not wearing the lifejacket — but my current situation makes it impossible for me to deny where the responsibility really lies. If I hadn't been drinking, I probably never would have flipped the boat.

I guess this time it looks like the right person has paid the price. I deserve to be paralyzed. I probably deserve worse. The panic I'd been feeling gives way to self-loathing and a sense of despair.

Drip, drip, drip.

As I lay there waiting for rescue, I see my life with an increasing clarity. All of the pain, all of the deceit, all of the suffering. For the first time, I'm able to stop thinking about myself and actually understand what I've been doing to everyone else. Tears overflow from my eyes as the full magnitude of the pain I've caused comes crashing in.

Drip, drip, drip.

I don't know how much time passes as I lay there mourning the time I've wasted and the suffering I've been responsible for. Eventually, a small glimmer of hope begins to flicker in my mind. *It doesn't have to be this way.*

'That's right. I can do better. As soon as I'm out of here, I'm going to turn things around. It won't be easy but I can do it.'

Drip, drip, drip.

Suddenly, light shines in and I can make out the web of cracks covering the shattered glass in front of me. I try to turn my head to get a view of the rest of the damage but I can't.

The light gets brighter and I see something beyond the shattered glass — something I can't quite make sense of: two large black lines, perhaps the silhouettes of my rescuers.

Drip, drip, tick.

The image in front of me sharpens a little as the light gets brighter. Everything is black and white. *That doesn't make sense.*

Tick, tick, tick.

There's a low rumble in the distance now. *Maybe the drip is rain and not leaking fuel. Is there a storm brewing out there?*

The silhouetted figures disappear and my mind immediately rejects what it sees.

No, this doesn't make any sense.

'Heh-heh-heh! Hello, Jordan. It's too late to repent now.'

No, it can't be!

Sammy's colossal malicious face grins back at me through the splintered glass, completely filling my vision.

Tick, tick, tick.

His laugh deepens. The light begins to grow dim again. A clock face rushes towards me as I start screaming uncontrollably.

Click.

Boleskine

By Michael Conroy

L'abbazia di Thèlema
Cefalù
Sicilia
1921

My Dear Sir,

Blessings from Baphomet. The Beast is grateful for your letter, although he would that his response was not so tardy. Sicilian peasants are to blame. The locals dare not approach us here on the hillside betwixt the olive trees. A rightfully superstitious lot, they refuse to deliver anything by hand, and so your correspondence remained at the post office for three weeks. They understand, it isn't wine we're making here.

It shames me that we are strangers, but I am glad to hear of our mutual acquaintance. How goes old Mr Mathers? I quite despise him, although a great deal less than the Order of the Golden Dawn entire. Weak men. All those so-called white magicians are, in truth, mere virginal charlatans. Especially that bookish Yeats. Nonetheless, I have surpassed their lot and it does me a disservice to dwell upon old grudges. I am, of course, happy to oblige your request. Love is the law, love under will.

I hereby enclose a set of instructions to which I urge you to adhere strictly. Follow the ritual from alpha to omega and make no mistake drawing the magickal seal. It is highly particular, and unlike anything scribbled in the *Ars Goetia.* I would go as far as to say that Messrs Dee and Kelley knew far less than my experience has imparted to me of the Dweller in the Abyss. Blood sacrifice will be required. And for your own protection, inscribe your triangle – set east of the circle – with the three names Tetragrammaton, Anaphaxeton and Primeumaton, along with the archangel Mi-Cha-El, divided thus by each corner.

Take no action until Venus enters Scorpio, and the moon is full and bright. As above, so below. I would also recommend fasting and meditation, to bolster the body and the spirit. We must master ourselves first, and then others. There are too many temptations to lead one astray here, much like in London. Discipline yourself, abstain from alcohol, heroin, cocaine, hashish, young boys, or any other stimulants; refrain from spilling your seed under any circumstances; and the fruits of your endeavours will be all the sweeter. Honour the ten sephiroth or prepare for total Ego death.

Proximity to nature only amplifies one's magickal potential. Ergo, I would divine a location with the requisite energies already in place. Flee the city, see the mountains, walk barefoot on the earth. Pity, had I never sold the place, I would gladly have invited you to Boleskine. It took me eleven months scouring Albion before I chanced upon her overlooking Loch Ness, as hard to find as any of my books were to publish. It's an old house full of unfinished business, for which I paid twice as much as it was worth and sold for even less. I suppose it stands empty now. Nobody sane would have gall enough to inhabit such a house. My heart often yearns to see it again, although my man Gillies lost his two children as recompense for my failed experiments.

Alas, Therion bids you adieu. Do what thou wilt shall be the whole of the law. Ra bestows upon his followers both tremendous victories and unimaginable torments. I took the liberty of casting the I-Ching on your behalf. Fortune is in your favour. If you ever find yourself in Sicilia for a honeymoon, do me the honour of visiting my Abbey. You may share the nightmare room.

Your friend,

***

Boleskine stood surrounded by trees on the south-east bank of Ness in the valley of Stratherrick. The journey took us seven hours from Glasgow – we practically flew there on twenty-five horsepower – but then again, time is an illusion. Fair as Ophelia, my beloved lay on the backseat, and not once did she stir (despite some squawking from an old potato sack). Lips parted, she would occasionally mumble, 'Mother, mother,' or something like that. Poor girl. Raised by her grandparents she was. They didn't mind me borrowing her though. Nor the office where she worked as a typist. It's not like we were strangers. We were soon to be married.

Low-hanging clouds perched over the hills around Tarff and Knockie as we trundled along through the dark. We passed a lonely church among the trees, and eventually, a little cemetery lit up in our headlamps signalled our arrival. I pulled off General Wade's Military Road, shut off the lights for obscurity's sake, and peered into the dark as we drove up the path.

Boleskine was no mansion – a single-storied hunting lodge shaped somewhat like the Hebrew letter ח. Yet it had more chimneys than a large family of woodcutters could reliably service. Between its two wings lay a gravelled courtyard bounded by a gate whose narrow path snaked away whence we'd come. Beside the gate, six stone steps rose to meet one of four vegetable gardens. The property was bounded by flat grassy lawns and hidden by several descending tiers of foliage to the north, beneath which the quiet expanse of the loch wrinkled like elephant skin. On the opposite bank, a sea of alders and ash trees swept up the hillside as though carpeting a vast mons pubis.

The full moon simmered from behind a passing cumulus. There were no lights on in the house as I pulled up before the gate. Beatrice lay on her side, wavy fondant hair scouring her shoulders, hands clasped like a penitent's. The chloroform was sure to buy me all the time I needed to prepare for the ceremony. I could have done with a sniff of the stuff myself on account of the poultry smell. 'Cluck-cluck,' the sack uttered by way of apology.

I shut off the engine and stepped out of the car. The quiet of the moors and high hills was broken only by the waves lapping the shore and the wind through the trees. I opened the gate and entered the courtyard. On a circular patch of land in the centre grew a cluster of saplings. Their young limbs shifted restlessly at my approach. I had an inkling that no one was home, although I couldn't help envisioning a caretaker with a blunderbuss just waiting for me to rear my head. I took a gander through the nearest window, but it was too dark to see anything inside.

Mr Crowley's failed experiments lingered in my mind. Black magick. What a load of codswallop. Don't believe everything you read in the papers. He'd wanted to confer with his Holy Guardian Angel, but the only way to accomplish such a high task was to first evoke and purge himself of the twelve Kings and Dukes of Hell. Six months it would have taken, according to Abramelin's method, but Mr Crowley had abandoned the house to assist Mr Mathers in some occult endeavour before he had been able to complete his great work. Whatever he'd managed to conjure up during those three months was in all likelihood still inhabiting the house, just waiting for the right magician to come along and bend it to his will. The house made an ideal setting for our elopement.

Thrice uttering the three names of God, I tried the door. Locked. I dug into my trouser pocket and pulled out a ring of skeleton keys. None of them worked on the big iron tumbler, so I quit their jingling, extracted my lockpick, and in no time at all—CLANK.

I meant only to open the door ajar, but a draught blew it full wide and left me gazing into pitch black. It took many long moments for my vision to adjust. The inner darkness left me with the impression not of an empty house bereft of occupants, but rather, of a colossal, pyramidal tomb.

'Hello?' I called, stepping back instinctively. I imagined eyes watching from the sidelight and transom, but it was nothing more than nerves. No ghostly apparition extended its clammy hand. No foaming Baskerville hound came charging out of the shadows. There was nothing but stillness. Funny how it's always in the dark you feel as though you're being watched.

Behind me, the car's headlamps clunked on, and drenched the courtyard in white light. I turned quickly and glimpsed four motionless figures beside the car. 'Who goes there?' I cried, rubbing my eyes, and registered the truth. Four shadows, nothing more. Beatrice had knocked the lights on and was now scarpering.

'Oh, bloody Nora!' I cursed, as she ran down the drive with her hands bound in front, but I'd been blessed with my mother's long gait, so I caught up to her no trouble and took her over my shoulder all romantic like.

'Let me go,' she screamed, her gag torn free. I told her to relax, but she knocked the wind out of me with a swift kick to the groin. That's one way to unblock your sacral chakra.

'Oof,' I groaned, and dropped to my knees beside the car.

She scrambled up again, but I grabbed her ankle, despite my glowing pain, and held her down.

'You're not making this easy,' I grunted.

'Fuck you,' she spat, and so I reached into the glove compartment, soaked another rag in chloroform, and held it over her mouth and nose for a good minute. By the time I took it away she was well and truly discombobulated. You've got to be careful with chloroform. Too much of the stuff might have killed her. 'Where am I?' she asked.

'You're in love,' I told her.

'Where's that then?' she giggled, and I had a flash of her picking daisies in a wet plate photograph. Fairies on her shoulders. Maybe we could take some pictures, I thought, hoisting her up and walking back towards the house. 'I'll be back for you shortly,' I told the potato sack.

'I had a little hen,' Beatrice said, 'the prettiest ever seen…'

I carried her over the threshold, and we found ourselves in a narrow entry hall. I lit a match and peered up and down the dark passage. Oriental carpets adorned the wooden floors. Frames hung on the walls missing their portraits. All the furniture had been covered by sheets.

The match burned down to my fingertips, so I shook it out and lit another. The flame twinkled in the glass eyes of a mounted deer head. And beyond that, the shadow of a door. My intuition seemed to desert me. At the opposite end of the corridor stood an identical door, but neither left nor right felt true. The house was a labyrinth, and we were mice.

In the cosy living room, I laid my beloved down on a sofa facing the fireplace.

'Gonna have your way with me then?' she asked too matter-of-factly for my liking.

'Don't talk so dirty like,' I told her. 'We're not yet married.'

I tried the switch for the electric light. Nothing. Those four figures stood watching us from the lawn outside, but they were still only shadows in the moonlight. Mr Scrooge's ghosts sprang to mind, and also, rather inexplicably, Mr Wells's Time Traveller. I shuddered, my arms and legs – and all my other extremities – tingling with anticipation, as I recalled a bizarre dream:

Four gay fellows in colourful military dress had visited me in my sleep and introduced themselves all by the same name. Pepper something, or something Pepper. Their leader, who distinguished himself only by a pair of small spectacles, was singing a strange song about marmalade skies and diamonds. There was a party going on too.

The air reeked of sweat and poppies, so I held a handkerchief over my mouth and nose. It was all so vivid like a Bosch painting. I didn't recognise a lot of faces, such was my limited education, but I remember spotting Marx and Jung, the spectre of Edgar Allan Poe, and Lawrence of Arabia, dagger on his belt, in his full white Bedouin costume. Each figure appeared as though he had been plucked from a stranger's imagination, portraits belonging to different artists.

Only one figure on the periphery seemed to acknowledge my presence. Wilde and Beardsley clung to him like twin girls to their father's coattails. Mr Crowley kept mum as the others jabbered to one another, and yet, in my mind, he spoke to me clear as a gramophone—

Something cooed in the fireplace, ruffled its wings, and fled up the chimney. It left a cloud of dust in its wake. I fixed on the hearth and waited. Nothing emerged. The room lapsed back into silence while we waited for the dust to settle. The match went out.

'Don't forget the chicken,' Beatrice coughed, wafting the air.

It was a rooster as it happens. Blood rushing to my temples, I jabbed my finger her way. 'You stay where you are, beautiful. I need my papers and tools. Then it's time to begin.'

The potato sack clucked miserably. 'I told you I'd come back for you,' I said, and checked all my magickal paraphernalia. Mr

Crowley's instructions, four candles, ritual dagger, and some sage for burning. I had no ceremonial vestments of silk, but my best shirt and jacket would fit the bill nicely.

Beatrice screamed and I hit my head on the car ceiling. Sack under one arm, doctor's bag under the other, I ran awkwardly back into the house, but she was waiting with a frying pan. CLANG. I hit the floor like a toppled column. My ears rang and shooting stars dazzled me. One side of my head throbbed, but I was lucky my nose hadn't been flattened.

She made the mistake of trying for a finishing blow, so I thwacked her before she could do me in. Soon I was on top of her, hand over her mouth, only for her to bite me, and I had no choice but to give her a good hard slap across the face. Then I threatened the girl with her own frying pan.

She'd somehow cut her bonds – lucky she hadn't come at me with a kitchen knife – so I bound her hands again. Ankles too this time. 'Der wobba fez! A fez obba boor,' she muttered through the dirty dishrag in her mouth.

I shook my head. 'A fez on a boar? You've been drinking, you have.'

She shook her head and spat out the gag. 'Oh God, it was rolling around like a ball…'

'Tall tales,' I said, stuffing the cloth back into her mouth, but then I heard it too. Something rolling and thumping over the ancient wooden floors. And so loudly. The house had the acoustics of a cathedral. THUMP. I looked up and down the corridor but saw nothing. THUMP. The door at the leftmost end of the passage loomed in the dark. Reaching into my bag of tricks, I dug out a candle, lit it, and started towards the door.

'Dodo! Gumbag!' Beatrice cried.

THUMP. The floorboards groaned under my weight as I strode past the deer head and stopped before the door. I reached for the handle but hesitated when the thumping stopped.

I tore it open, not knowing what to expect. A rat? A pigeon? A severed head? I found the bedroom empty. No sheets, no mattress, only a rickety frame. I swallowed at the sight of a wet black stain on the wall around head height. Damp? Mould? The smell of smoke lingered in the air.

An identical door leading to a study and a library revealed itself at a right angle to the bedroom. The study was lit by a large bay window, and there was a little door that opened out onto the garden. Stripped to its skeleton, even the floorboards were bare, and only a cushioned armchair remained. The space was ample, and the atmosphere electric. It was perfect. I was quite certain it was the room in which Mr Crowley had worked all those years ago. And now, I mused, it would be our church.

Beatrice was halfway out the door when I returned. She hadn't the least warmth to spare, although the fairer sex does often play coy. 'Don't get cold feet on me now,' I said, and gave her a fireman's lift to the study, not forgetting my bag of tricks, and, of course, the sacrificial rooster.

The bird beat its wings as I lifted it out of the sack. Setting foot on the floor, it made an immediate beeline for the exit, but finding the door closed, gave up all hope of escape and strutted about at ease. 'Cluck-cluck,' it said passively, and pecked a beetle off the floor.

Beatrice watched it with a fallen look on her face. Neither she nor the rooster would be leaving before the night was done.

I drew the triangle set east of the magickal circle just as Mr Crowley had said. *The Lesser Key of Solomon* called for a coiled serpent inscribed with Hebrew letters to be drawn inside, surrounding four hexagrams with a central rhombus on which the magician should stand. Everything was to be drawn in chalk or painted on the floor. I'm no artist, so I substituted the snake for a handful of all-purpose magickal words instead: *Elohim, Abracadabra, Bibbidi-Bobbidi-Boo*. You couldn't go wrong with those. Then I drew four pentagrams outside the circle, lit four candles, and burned sage to ward off negative energy. Nothing scuppers a business deal like a bad odour.

The final addition was to draw the seal of Choronzon inside

the triangle. I shan't bother describing the madness that Mr Crowley had sketched for me, but it could only have been drawn by a man at once totally enlightened and doped up higher than a tribal shaman. You might say it was the calling card of Chaos itself. I thought on what he'd written to me. *Prepare for total Ego death*. A tot of gin would have calmed my nerves. Bloody abstinence.

I began with the preliminary invocation: 'Thee I invoke, the Bornless one. Thee that didst create the Earth and the Heavens. Thee that didst create the Day and the Night. Thee that didst create the Dark and the Light…'

Beatrice mumbled unintelligibly, so I pulled out the dishrag and let her speak freely. 'You're mad, you are,' she said, lying on her back. 'There are plenty of nice girls in Bedlam you could have...' She laughed. 'Listen to me, trying to talk sense to a madman… Oh God, please don't sacrifice me to the Devil.'

'Nobody's sacrificing anyone, my love.' The rooster clucked chasing a spider. 'Except for him, that is, but he's just poultry.' I picked the rooster up with both hands and cradled him under my armpit. 'I've watched you for a long time, Beatrice. I know everything about you. The first time I saw you, all those years ago, I knew that we would one day be together.'

Her face dropped. 'Aren't you the butcher's boy? Yes, I remember now. We went to school together. Didn't Mickey Noonan drop a frog down your pants once?'

I drew the ritual dagger from my belt. 'I am a servant of the Most-High and nothing less.'

Facing east towards the empty triangle, I stood in my power at the centre of the circle, while Beatrice looked on in awe of my impressive dagger. Or perhaps my rooster.

The moon poured in through the window. It was a quarter to midnight by the time I'd completed all the preparations. I waited until the witching hour before beginning the first conjuration: 'I do invocate and conjure thee, O Spirit Choronzon; and with power armed from the Supreme Majesty,

I do strongly command, invoke, and conjure thee...'

It was all very long-winded and had no effect. Not even a shiver up the spine. The temperature in the room remained chilly, but not uncomfortable. The rooster bobbed its head.

Beatrice rolled her eyes. 'Whatever you're trying to do isn't going to work. Oh, I don't care, I just want to go home. If you let me go, I promise I won't tell anyone about this.'

I ignored her and recited the second conjuration: 'I do invocate, conjure, and command thee, O thou Spirit Choronzon, to appear and to show thyself visibly unto me before this circle in fair and comely shape...' I waved my dagger and visualised the spirit's coming, but the triangle remained empty.

Mr Crowley had intimated to me that the Dweller in the Abyss might well be a pain in the arse, so I pressed on with the constraint and the general curse: 'O thou wicked and disobedient Spirit Choronzon, because thou hast rebelled, and hast not obeyed nor regarded my words which I have rehearsed, I curse thee into the depths of the Bottomless Abyss...'

I felt a sudden vibrational change in the air. Resistance. So I made him an offering: 'O Spirit, I humbly bid that you accept this offering of a comely rooster. May its lifeblood satiate and persuade thee to appear before me. Behold!'

The chicken squawked as I slit its throat. Blood spilled onto the floor and its body went limp. Then I cast it out of the circle beside the triangle, and waited for the spirit to act, but the spirit was stubborn. 'Ungrateful swine. That was a prize cock, that was.'

I wiped the blood onto my trousers. What next? Press on with the conjuration of the fire? The invocation of the King? The greater curse? I thought back on all my prior attempts at conjuration. Failures. It couldn't have all been for nothing. I wouldn't have drugged and kidnapped the girl had I not had some certainty of success. How else was she going to love me?

Beatrice stared at me like I was loony. 'Whose throat will

you slit next?'

I scratched the back of my head. 'Perhaps, I should have brought two chickens... Let's try it again. I can prick my finger for a drop of blood.'

I repeated all the aforementioned steps, but when it came time to offer a new sacrifice, I said unto the spirit, 'If you doubt my dedication, please look to the dead rooster on the floor, and to my own blood which I spill here for you now.' I pricked the tip of my pointer with the dagger and squeezed out a few drops of the red stuff.

Bloody nothing. The air remained still, candles burning, triangle empty. It was two in the morning by this time. All that fasting had done me no good whatsoever. A nice fry-up would have hit the spot right about then. Beatrice was looking pale too. In fact, she'd fallen asleep inside the circle. I had nothing to lose, so I repeated the ritual one more time, but instead of merely pricking my finger, I slit open my mount of Venus and flicked the blood out of the circle.

The four candles guarding the four cardinal points flickered as though recoiling from a sudden draught, and then, as though someone had turned up the gas, each flame shot up like a firework and spread wetly across the ceiling. The fire dissipated quickly, but the ceiling was scorched. I dropped the dagger and it landed hilt up like Excalibur.

The air inside the triangle swirled and gathered unto itself like a dust devil.

'Now we're getting somewhere,' I grinned, while Beatrice, oblivious to my success, carried on snoring open-mouthed at my feet.

The cyclone did not acknowledge me, so I addressed it first: 'Art thou the Spirit Choronzon?'

A voice in my head replied affirmatively. 'Choronzon.'

'I have conjured thou here to assist me with matters of the heart.' I nodded towards the sleeping Beatrice. 'I wish that she would love me.'

The spirit repeated itself. 'Choronzon.'

'I command you to – I don't know how it works – change her mind, influence her, or something. Make her love me as I love her. Marriage, a couple of kids, the works.'

'Choronzon.'

'Oh bloody stop, will you? I'm not here to play games. I've gone to all this trouble, it's three in the morning, and I'm tired, so make the girl love me!'

'Fat chance,' Beatrice said, and threatened me with the dagger. 'I don't know what's going on, but I'm leaving. You can stay here and rot.' I moved towards her, but she swiped the blade at me, and stepped back towards the edge of the circle. 'Try to stop me and I'll make you less of a man than you are now.'

I raised my hands. 'You can't leave the circle. It's not safe out there. You don't understand.'

Wasted words. The spirit took her the moment she stepped foot beyond the boundary. She swiped the dagger left and right as though fending off a swarm of bees, but it was useless. There was no escape from the cyclone as it sprouted a mass of tendrils and reached up her nose and down her throat until she'd swallowed it all. Convulsions contorted her body at first, but then she stopped still. Hunched over with her back to me, she adopted a spider-like pose with both hands flat on the floor.

'Beatrice?'

In my grandmother's voice, she sighed, 'No Beatrice here,' before her head snapped back, and she stood upright. It was then that I noticed all her clothes had changed. Not only her clothes, but her entire body had been transformed. *Something* had replaced her.

It turned to face me.

The redhaired creature that had taken her place had two different coloured eyes. The left eye was hazel, its pupil permanently dilated, while the right eye shone pale blue in the candlelight. On its forehead was a painted gold medallion like a third eye wide open. It wore a striped jacket with a spread collar – exposing a smooth, sinewy chest – matching pants, which it wore without braces, and knee-high red leather boots. It stood between me and the garden. My only means of escape was back through the house.

At first, it said nothing, and only eyed me curiously from afar. Moonlight glinted off the blade in its slender hand. Then, stepping towards me, and retracting its red lips into a bone white snarl, the thing serenaded me with the words, '*There's nothing you can do...*'

Recoiling, I stumbled over one of my candles, hit the floor, and shuffled backwards.

The thing laid one hand against its cheek and sang, '*I could lick you by smiling... I could leave you to hang...*'

I tore open the door and heaved it shut again. The creature tried the handle, so I held fast, pulling on it with all my weight, and after a long moment, it stopped.

Panting, I walked backwards across the bedroom towards the corridor, when the handle turned, and the door creaked open ajar.

Its pale blue eye gleamed in the dark. '*Oh, you pretty thing.*'

I ran for the front entrance, but the door wouldn't budge, no matter how I wrestled with the knob. Peaking out into the corridor, I heard it scream, '*Five years stuck on our eyes!*'

A whiff of smoke tickled my nose, but its origin remained a mystery. Fire and brimstone, most likely. I held my breath and crept along the passage towards the eastmost door. Inside, a skinny bearded wild man jumped up from his desk in fright. He'd been writing music, poring over notes and bars. There were many scrunched-up sheets filling a wastepaper basket on the floor.

'Who the hell are you?' he gasped, clutching a queer guitar like a medieval axe. He wore denim jeans, a loose-fitting plaid shirt, and leather boots. There was a young girl, no more than fourteen, asleep on the sofa – half-dressed, she stirred at the sound of our exchange, but didn't wake.

The conversation felt surreal. 'Get thee behind me, spirit,' I warned him. 'I've had enough grief off your lot this evening.'

'Get out or I'll call the police!' the musician said. 'Don't you know who I am?' His full beard and shaggy hair made him the spitting image of Christ – that is, if Christ had been a cowboy.

I didn't fancy explaining myself to the rozzers, so I dashed through the dining room, into the kitchen, and dived out the window onto the lawn. There was no way home besides the car, so I cranked her up like a fisherman on ayahuasca. Smoke stung my eyes – the smell and taste of it were overpowering – but it was only as I reversed down the drive that I saw the flames. The entire house had erupted in a conflagration, black smoke rising chimney-like into the sky. And so black was the smoke, so opaque, that it blotted out the moon and the stars.

My plans had been scuppered, so I drove far and fast, and not once did I glance over my shoulder – for fear that the house might draw me back. Now I understand why Mr Crowley never returned to Boleskine. Too much unfinished business. Business to which I, myself, have certainly contributed. I still wonder about that musician, and the *thing* that possessed poor Beatrice. Ziggy. Something Ziggy was its name. It still haunts my dreams. The doctors don't believe me, but I'm no fool. I know all about the Homo superior, and the man who fell to Earth. It's the spiders who are the cause of it all: there are spiders *living on Mars.*

Behind the Mask

By Isabella Hunter

Akane had grown used to spending long periods alone while her husband, Soma Moritane, was away. She would stay at Odaka Castle while he was in the north ensuring the Date clan couldn't push into the Soma territory. Akane was satisfied with being married to the head of the Soma clan, even if they were a small clan compared to the neighbouring territories, and she had no intention of putting her position at risk.

She would play the good wife to Moritane. Akane knew she was beautiful. The rest she had perfected through years of practice. She could entertain guests all day long with songs and dances. Akane was proficient in all the skills of a dutiful wife, not that she had needed to do any cooking or cleaning since becoming a Soma.

However, the talents that Akane was the proudest of were her war skills. She'd trained to be a worthy general, one that could one day lead the Soma clan. She had worked with both bow and sword until she could best the strongest warriors she could find. She knew all the clans throughout the land and where their allegiances lay. Akane knew she needed all of these combined if she was to carve a name for herself like the great Tomoe Gozen had.

With Moritane away, Akane had free reign of the castle and the surrounding town. Now, she pulled on a brilliant red irotomesode with embroidered flowers flowing around her lower half for the trip into the town. The sun shone through the new leaves sprouting from the trees, hinting at summer's approach. A light breeze blew through the streets, carrying with it cherry blossoms.

Akane always enjoyed going into the town. She wanted the people to think of her as more than just Moritane's wife. She wanted them to think of her as a reliable leader and someone they could trust. Akane waved as she passed the townsfolk, nodding to an elderly couple sat on a bench. She wanted to stop and talk with them but today she had an appointment she couldn't afford to miss. She walked through the streets, keeping the sweet smile upon her face, all the way to the blacksmith.

The blacksmith's was a large, stone building with a tall chimney. Akane pushed open the door leading into the store front. It was a clean room filled with shining weapons of all kinds. However, there was a lot of smoke in the air, issuing from a curtained passage way. Even at this distance, Akane's skin prickled from the heat of the workshop. The clang of metal on metal echoed from the room at the back. 'Excuse me?' Akane called over the din.

The hammering stopped. Akane waited. A young man pushed the curtain aside and came up to the counter. He was wearing thick leather all over. His face was the only part exposed, the skin glistening with sooty sweat. His black hair was pulled tight, keeping it out of his eyes. 'Akane, I'm glad you could make it,' he said. 'I have the sword in the back. I'll go get it now.'

He disappeared behind the curtain, returning a moment later with the katana. 'Here she is,' he said, offering it up with both hands.

Akane felt the weight in her hands and examined the keen edge of the blade. The rope work on the handle was soft and even against her palms. The hand-guard was an intricate lattice of metal work. 'It's beautiful,' she said softly. 'Will you be able to deliver it to the castle tomorrow?'

'Absolutely, I just want to do the final polish and refinements,' he nodded, as he took the sword back. 'I'll have it to you in the morning. I hope Daimyo Soma will love it. She really is my finest work.'

'Perfect. I'll see you then.'

She left the blacksmith, straightening out her irotomesode and brushing soot from her shoulders. All the preparations were now in place for her husband's return tomorrow.

The guards at the castle gate greeted her with a simple nod, opening the wooden door without a word. The castle didn't have a large number of staff. There were only enough to keep it running. She climbed the stairs up to the castle's main building.

She pushed open the door and found her husband kneeling in the entranceway. He was dressed in his full armour, clutching his sword. His body shook with violent tremors. His helmet cast a dark shadow over his face, obscuring it from view. 'Darling, you're home! I wasn't expecting you back until tomorrow evening. Is everything okay?'

'I left my second-in-command in charge, to return home early,' he spat, as though he had eaten something rotten.

'That's great. Why don't we celebrate with a drink?' she asked, taking a careful step into the room.

Moritane's hand tightened on his sword hilt. Akane froze, watching him. 'I bet you'd like that. You have a life of luxury while spreading your legs for every man who takes your fancy while I'm away.'

'I don't know what you mean!'

'I saw you in town, leaving the blacksmith's.'

'I think you have misunderstood. Let me explain–'

'Enough! I've had it with your lies,' he boomed. 'Everyone in town knows about your visits to the smith. They're laughing at me!' His shoulders were shaking. Akane couldn't make out if he had begun to laugh or sob. He stilled, releasing a slow breath.

'I was going to–'

'Shut your mouth, whore!' His sword suddenly came free.

There was a flash of white across Akane's vision. She looked down but her body had no signs of being struck. Droplets of blood spattered onto the floor at her feet. She could feel blood gushing down her face and into her mouth. She tasted a metallic tang of it.

She reached up to her face. She was cut from ear to ear in a grotesque caricature of a smile. Her face was hot. Her breath came ever faster and darkness tinged her vision. Akane took a step forward, reaching out towards her husband. He struck again, this time plunging his sword through her stomach. Akane looked down at the blade stuck in her midriff. Her legs gave way beneath her and she fell to the floor.

***

Akane awoke. Her body was cold and stiff. Even opening her eyes was a challenge. She finally managed it and peered around. She winced at the pain every movement of her head caused. Moist leaf litter softened the compacted dirt under her body. Akane stared up at the bizarre place in which she'd awoken. Above her, black, leafless trees reached towards a blood red sky unlike anything she'd ever seen.

She pushed herself up. Her stomach protested at the movement. She examined her clothes. She was no longer in her red irotomesode; instead she was in the shinishozoku of the deceased. The fabric was stained red over her middle. She touched the blood, remembering Moritane piercing her.

The forest was devoid of any signs of life, the trees looking burnt or rotten. There was no sound, no birds chirping, only a dead silence. A pearly white moon shone down from above the trees, giving everything an eerie glow. Far off in the distance, blue lights flickered. Akane felt drawn towards them. She should flee the flames of yokai, but looking around the empty forest Akane knew she had no choice.

The blue wisps disappeared as she approached, and more flickered into life further away, leading her through the trees. The forest thinned and, on the horizon, Akane saw a colossal city reaching into the crimson sky. Large walls encased the city, the only opening a bent and broken torii gate. Akane saw two hulking figures to either side of the gate. One was a large bipedal horse and the other was a bull, each with only a cloth tied around their groins.

Akane approached them cautiously. She had no weapon to defend herself with if they showed signs of aggression. The sheer size of the beasts only became apparent once she'd drawn closer. She was forced to tip her head back just to meet the gaze of Ox and Horse, as she looked from one to the other. All was silent, save for the heavy breathing of Ox, and Horse pawing the soil with his hooves.

'Someone really did a number on your face,' Ox grunted. 'You look horrifying.'

Akane lifted her sleeve, covering the slash over her mouth. 'How do I get out of this place?' she asked. 'I have unfinished business.'

'Don't we all?' snorted Ox.

'Only way you are getting out of here is if the Demon Lord allows it,' Horse whinnied.

'Tell me where he is then,' Akane responded.

Horse pointed through the gate to a fortress that put Odaka castle to shame. 'The Demon Lord resides in the castle at the centre of the city. Just follow this road and it will lead you to the entrance.'

The pair moved aside, allowing her to pass through the gate. The buildings beyond were painted in the hues of bruises, all dark blues, greens, purples, and reds. It was nothing like the town she had lived in before. Lamps were strung along the street filled with the same blue flames that had led her from the forest.

The people in the street were the strangest sight of all though. There was a woman with a neck that stretched up past the roofs. A sentient straw parasol hopped down the road on a human leg. Green-skinned kappa ran past her legs, chattering among themselves, harassing a store clerk selling cucumbers.

Faces turned to her the further she moved through the street towards the castle. They grimaced at the sight of her face. She covered her mouth again, but the stares continued, following her down the road. Each person pushed her to move faster towards her destination.

The walls of the castle loomed in front of Akane. Her phantom heart pounded against her chest. She traced the slash across her face, wincing in shame. Akane couldn't allow the Demon Lord to see her like this if she was going to implore him into allowing her to go kill her husband. Akane looked for some way to cover her mouth, but she only had the clothes she was wearing.

She looked down at the long, flowing sleeves of her shinishozoku. She bit down on the thin fabric and tore a piece free. She tied a mask for herself across the lower half of her face.

Akane moved to the entrance of the castle. A deep red bridge connected the castle to the rest of the city. Akane crossed in a tense silence, dreading what it would be to come face to face with the Demon Lord. She stepped off the wooden boards onto the castle grounds.

Giant doors stood open in front of her. Blue flame illuminated the room ahead. Akane peered inside. The large room was empty except for a dark wooden desk in the centre, but there was no sign of any attendant. She pushed forward, checking every alcove carefully for signs of life. There was no one in the entrance hall except for herself.

Akane moved to the the desk. It was bare except for a golden bell set to one side. She scanned the room once more. She tapped the bell, wincing as its loud, summoning tone echoed through the building.

A column of azure flame shot up behind the desk. As it

dissipated, a gargantuan man was revealed. He was seated in full crimson armour, his face obscured by a hannya mask. However, the horns that protruded from the mask were all too real, two jagged spires of lapis lazuli curling towards the ceiling.

Akane resisted the desire to step back from him, bracing her legs against the stone floor. The man sat in silence, staring at her. Akane couldn't judge him with his face hidden behind the mask. She steeled herself. If she wanted vengeance upon her husband she needed to get this oni to help her. 'My name is Soma Akane. I wish to be sent back to the human realm. I must kill my husband.'

The oni slapped a massive hand on the desk. His body was trembling. He sucked in a deep breath, and then released thunderous laughter. Akane shifted uncomfortably, waiting for the oni to cease his howling. Finally, his body stilled as he gazed at Akane. 'Listen, you'd be pretty if you took off that rag, and I'm sure you're used to people bending over backward for you,' he said. 'But I don't just hand out access to the human realm. I'll need something in exchange, if you know what I mean.'

Akane chose to ignore his crude and suggestive tone. 'I am a skilled swordsman and an excellent strategist. I was married to a daimyo so I'm familiar with running a town. I'm sure I can be of use to you.'

'Maybe I can find some work for you but you'll need to prove yourself before I let you go swanning out of here. Go speak with Kenzo. He'll be able to set you up with some work and, if you prove yourself worth my while, I'll consider allowing you access to the human realm.'

Determination filled her. She nodded to the Demon Lord. 'I'll prove myself to you, be sure of that. Where can I find Kenzo?'

'You can find him in the room down the far end of that corridor.' He jabbed a thumb towards the arched hallway to his left. 'I look forward to hearing about your work. But if you do reconsider my other offer feel free to visit me in my room.'

Akane's skin crawled at the very suggestion. Before she had

a chance to rebuff him, however, blue flames consumed the Demon Lord's body and Akane was alone once more.

The hallway was long and dark, with doors lining either side, but at the far end light came from a door that was slightly ajar. Akane approached, conscious of her footsteps echoing down the corridor. Voices and laughter grew louder the closer she got. She stopped short of the room.

She peeked inside. There was all different types of yokai socialising at a long table. Ghosts in shinishozoku, like herself, hulking beasts, and even a beautiful spider woman stretched across several chairs. Akane's hand drifted to the cloth she'd tied around her face. She tightened the knot and pushed the door open.

Every face in the room turned towards her at once. She felt their assessing gazes, as they sized her up. Akane breathed deeply through her nose. 'I'm looking for Kenzo,' she announced. 'The Demon Lord told me to speak with him.'

A giant toad pushed itself up from its chair, raising a webbed hand to Akane. 'That would be me,' Kenzo croaked. 'What's he sent you for?'

Akane kept her eyes on Kenzo, but felt the pressure of the silence around her. 'I'm going to be working for him from today.' Now she made eye contact with each of the different yokai sat around the table. 'I look forward to working with you all,' she said.

The reactions varied around the room. Most gave her a brief nod of acknowledgement, or ignored her by staring down at the table. The spider woman didn't flinch from Akane's gaze, though. Instead, the woman gave her a smile, and casually waved one of her black spider legs.

'Come with me and I'll get you some equipment,' Kenzo said, as he came around the table and went past her, out into the hallway. His bare feet slapped the floor with each step, leaving a slimy residue in their wake. Akane followed him into the corridor, letting Kenzo pull the door shut behind them. He moved to a metal door, unlocking it with iron keys chained to his sash.

The room beyond was filled with shelves lined with clothes, weapons of all types, and bottles of various shapes and sizes.

'We'll get you kitted up and find some work for you. Do you want something better to keep your mouth covered?"

'I'd appreciate that,' Akane answered.

Kenzo pulled a stack of red clothing down and handed it over to Akane. He bent down and grabbed a small slip of black cloth with a pair of fabric ties from a box. He put it onto of the pile Akane was holding. 'That should work better for you,' he said, patting the black cloth. 'It's a simple face mask. We use them anytime we have work to do that the Demon Lord would rather keep anonymous. I hope you don't have any lingering morality, because things can get dirty.'

'I don't care what work I'm doing. I just want to get working as soon as possible so the Demon Lord will let me go to the human realm.'

Kenzo's face scrunched as much as his warty skin allowed. 'I don't know what he said to you, but he isn't going to let you go to the human realm. At least, he never let me.' Kenzo's voice trailed off, and his head dropped.

'Has he ever let anyone go?' Akane asked. She looked down at the pile of clothes in her arms.

'Not that I've ever seen, and I've been here for a couple of hundred years.'

'Do you know if he can actually travel between realms?'

'I've seen him do it before, but he keeps the mirror he uses locked in his bedroom.' Kenzo's expression was unreadable. 'What's your weapon of choice?'

'I'm best with a medium length sword.'

Kenzo moved to the back of the room where sheathed swords, naginata, and other assorted weapons were kept. He picked up a sword, turning it over in his hand, and passed it to Akane. 'You will be needing this. I'll take you to your room.

There is a nice one that's free, down the hall from the Demon Lord's room actually.'

Akane nodded. 'That sounds perfect.'

'I'll escort you to your room, then.'

Akane followed Kenzo through the stone hallway and up to the top floor of the castle. On the higher levels, the corridors were decorated with deep red carpets running the lengths of them. Kenzo slowed at a door, unlocking it with a key from his chain. 'If you need anything you can find the boss just two doors down.' He pointed to an ornate set of double doors down the hallway.

'Thank you. I'll be sure to call on him if needed.' Akane moved into the room, waving goodbye to Kenzo before pulling the door shut. The room was decorated with splendid wooden furniture and plush throws and cushions. Akane unfolded the clothes she had been given. They were a dark red hakama and kimono similar to what she wore for training.

She unwrapped her obi, letting her shinishozoku pool on the ground around her feet. A mirror at the far end of the room flashed at her. She walked to the mirror, standing in front of it, wearing only the scrap of cloth tied around her face. She unravelled it, revealing the long gash her husband had left her with.

The skin at the corners of her lips were split open up to her ears. Blood was dried around the wound and dark scabs crusted around the edges of the slice. Akane opened her mouth, peering in at the unobstructed view of her teeth and gums. She turned away from the sight of her mutilated face, busying herself with donning the clothing Kenzo had given her.

Once dressed, and having smoothed out the lines of the hakama, Akane put on the new cloth mask. It covered the gaping maw that was now her mouth. She turned her face to the mirror, ensuring that none of the wound was visible. She pulled her hair out from under the mask, letting it cascade over her shoulders.

Akane slipped her sword's sheath through her the fabric looped around her waist. She pulled the blade free, testing the feel of it slicing through the air. It weighed on her arm more than the swords she was used to but she would only need it for one strike. Akane sheathed the sword again, satisfied.

She felt her smile reach her eyes, even if under the mask her lips resembled a snake ready to strike. She left her room, keeping relaxed and balanced as she moved towards the door Kenzo had pointed out. She flowed forwards, overwhelming her every instinct to turn back.

The massive wooden doors in front of Akane reminded her of just how insignificant her size seemed in comparison to the Demon Lord. Her hand hovered inches from the door for a long moment. She looked back at the room she'd come from. Why couldn't she just start over and forget her husband had ever existed. Her gut twisted at the thought. Not only had he made her into this monster in his own mind, but also in this afterlife, ensuring she would never know peace. Even the yokai grimaced at the sight of her.

She knocked on the door three times. 'Whoever it is, you'd better have a good reason for disturbing me,' the Demon Lord called from beyond.

'It's Soma Akane. I have reconsidered your offer.'

A deep rumbling laugh issued from the room. 'Have you, now? I knew a pretty girl like yourself would know what she was good for.' There was a rustling and stomping, before the door swung open to reveal the Demon Lord still wearing his hannya but while only in a thin robe. Dark red skin showed from underneath his clothes. His head was covered in thick, white hair that fell to his chest in wild curls.

Akane suppressed a shudder at his words. 'Do you really think I'm pretty?'

The Demon Lord rubbed a hand over his red mask, humming to himself. 'I'm glad you've reconsidered. I do think you're pretty. I'm sure you would be prettier if you took off your clothes, though.'

Akane reached up, untying the straps holding her mask over her lips. The cloth fell to the floor. 'How about now? Do you still think I'm pretty?'

The Demon Lord's purr turned into a strangled retch. 'That's disgusting. No wonder you keep yourself covered up. Get out of here.' He shooed at her with one hand, keeping the other firmly clasped over his mask.

'That's a shame,' Akane mumured, running a finger along the edge of her cut. 'I thought we could come to some kind of arrangement. But if this isn't suitable, I guess we can figure something else out.' She grabbed her sword, pulling it from the sheath in one fluid movement. The blade cut deep across the Demon Lord, slicing through his robes into his gut.

He fumbled his innards as they spilled free. Then he wobbled and collapsed to his knees before falling onto his back. Akane reached out and snapped the hannya mask off him. The face beneath was more boar than human, tusks stretching his lips beneath an upturned nose. He sneered at her, blood trickling from his lips. His eyes glazed and he moved no more.

Akane turned the mask over in her hand. It was a hannya used to depict a jealous female demon. Akane ran her fingers over the scowling lips, appreciating the anger captured exquisitely in the wood. She raised her sword, and struck the mask in two. She tied the lower half around her own face.

Stepping over the Demon Lord's body, she entered the room. It was massive, and double the size of her own, with rich tapestries covering every wall. The plush carpet underfoot soaked up the blood spreading from the Demon Lord's body. There was a full-length mirror at the far end of the room. The silver surface undulated like the waves of the ocean.

Akane saw herself reflected in the rippling mirror, but behind her reflection was not the opulent room of the Demon Lord. It was her home that she saw, her home before she had been killed: Odaka Castle. Akane reached out. She pushed her fingers into the mirror. A chill crept through her as she reached deeper into the mirror.

She felt herself being pulled forwards, knowing beyond the mirror she would find her husband. She would be able to show him what he had done to her and do the same to him. Akane scrunched her eyes closed as she stepped through. The cold that overtook her made her gasp. She opened her eyes, blinking against the blinding sight of Odaka Castle covered in a thick layer of snow.

Akane went to the entrance, snow crunching beneath her feet. There were no guards posted. She flexed her hands against the biting cold. She stood before the familiar, wooden doors. Her heart hammered in her chest as she pushed them wide.

Muffled voices drifted to her from within the castle. A woman's voice. An unfamiliar woman's voice. She was cooing in a room on the second floor. Akane climbed the stairs without a sound. A beam of light shone from an open door down the hall. Akane came to the door and peeped through.

A woman sat on a chair, cradling a baby to her bare chest. Her clothes were simple but well made, not the type of clothes a wetnurse would wear. Akane leaned further around the door, trying to get a clear view of the woman's face. A floorboard creaked under her foot. The woman's head came up. She jumped to her feet, clutching the child. 'Please don't hurt my baby,' she pleaded, as the infant began to mewl.

Akane held her hands up, showing she was unarmed. 'I'm not after you or your child. I'm looking for Soma Moritane.'

'What do you want with my husband?'

Akane looked from the woman to the child. 'Your husband? Soma Moritane is *my* husband. I am Soma Akane.'

'Akane died years ago,' the woman yelped. 'If you are Akane, that would make you a yurei. Some kind of demon.' The woman was backing away from Akane with each word.

Akane touched her mask. 'I guess you could say that. I don't have time for this. Tell me where Moritane is.'

'He should be in his bedroom.' The woman pointed the way, but Akane was already leaving: She knew the way.

He was hunched over his desk, working through papers. 'Do you think I'm pretty?' she asked from the door.

Moritane whipped around in his chair to face her. 'Akane? Is that you?' he asked, aghast, pushing up from his seat. The wrinkles around his eyes were deeper than she remembered.

'I asked you a question.'

'It is, isn't it?' He moved towards her, reaching out to her face. Akane froze in place as he unfastened the ties, letting the hannya drop to the floor with a clatter. 'I'm so sorry for what I did to you. The blacksmith arrived with my sword the day after I...' He trailed off, staring at the cut splitting her face open.

Akane swallowed, trying not to hear his words. 'I've come here to have my vengeance upon you, my retribution. I'm going to do to you what you did to me.' Her fingers twitched towards her sword.

Moritane dropped to his knees. 'I accept my fate,' he said abjectly. 'I welcome it, even. It will be a relief.' He held her gaze, unashamed of his tears, as she drew her sword from its sheath.

'I will be swift,' she promised. Yet a baby's cry echoed from down the hall, pulling her attention from the man who had once been her husband. 'I will be–' She stopped. Slowly, she returned her sword to its sheath. 'I would not have my vengeance bring you any sort of relief. And I would not see the child suffer unfairly for the loss of its father. But know yourself cursed, Moritane – for I will be waiting for you beyond this world.'

Moritane's went over Akane's shoulder, and Akane became aware that the woman with her child had witnessed the whole scene. 'I wish a happy and peaceful life to both you and your child. What did you name the infant?' Akane asked.

'This is Soma Yoshitane,' the woman whispered.

'Be sure to raise him as a fine man, and a *better* one than his father! Also, be in no doubt that I will be watching from the demon realm. My vengeance will never be far away.'

The Shadow in the Lightning

By Matt Beeson

Darmstadt

It was 2005. I had been born twenty-three years earlier, in Darmstadt, Germany. I was schooled in Darmstadt, I grew up in Darmstadt, and I studied at the University in Darmstadt. I graduated with honours at both undergraduate level and postgraduate level. I briefly considered a life outside of the university with a girl who ultimately left me for an American. I returned to read a PhD in planetary sciences, specialising in exometeorology. I was young, bright and full of ideas, and yet oddly afraid of leaving Darmstadt. It seemed inevitable that almost immediately upon completion of my doctorate I should take the steady stroll, past the hauptbahnhoff, to work on the other side of the city at the European Space Agency.

My metaphorical stroll continued to the Cassini/Huygens project mission control room early on the morning of 14th January. I was on my best behaviour, an early night previously, along with a healthy but light breakfast. The ink on my PhD final paper still damp – figuratively, you understand, we had laptops in 2005 – I felt immeasurably privileged to be there watching as Huggie began his descent. Suffice it to say that I expected to have very little to contribute. It came, therefore, as something of a surprise when shortly after 11:17am – the parachutes were open – Emilia looked up at me from the control floor and beckoned me to come down from the gallery.

Professor Emilia Schulze, my academic supervisor was an amazing human being. She'd been with Cassini/Huygens since project inception. She was always keen to help me develop, because of my interest and burgeoning expertise in a nascent field, and because we were two women together in what was still then a man's world. Emilia and I had become closer than either of us would have wished to declare publically, although since she passed I feel more comfortable speaking of our mutual regard. It was complicated but, needless to say, it didn't harm my career. Kurzgesagt, I still feel, without false modesty, that Emilia is the main reason I came to be in the operations centre, mission control, for the Huygens probe as it landed on Titan. Huggie was on Titan; I was in Darmstadt.

Greeting me at the foot of the gallery steps, smiling, arm on the small of my back, Emilia explained to me that Huggie was being carried along by high altitude winds at over one hundred metres per second! 'You might be needed to consult,' she said with a wink. I could barely keep the grin from my face. Despite the weather, we were not anxious. We had confidence in the rugged little probe. Huggie was prepared for most landing eventualities but, as it transpired, the landing was to be the least of it.

I was, I am, a scientist, and I am German. I pride myself on my capacity for objectivity, yet despite or because of these sensibilities, it never ceases to amaze me the extent to which we grow fond of these little robotic fellows. I shed a tear or two, we all did, when Cassy finally slipped beneath the clouds. That night Sascha and I hat zu viel getrunken: whiskey, not my usual alt bier. But that was twelve years after Titan, after *the beginning of the end of the world.* You may wonder if I'm being too dramatic, but I don't think I am. Some will later nod sagely wise and say something about how Titan changed everything; it's just that nobody noticed at the time. Others might say that Titan was just the tip of the iceberg, how it had all started one hundred years earlier, or five hundred years earlier. It always depends on your point of view.

Huggie had landed successfully. The controller beckoned to the SOM and I understood that the camera feed was coming through. There I was, on the floor of the control centre just as the first pictures from the surface of Titan were arriving at earth from one billion miles away! Soon a small crowd had developed around the SOM and the repeater screen. The smiles and excitement had given way to concerned expressions; now there was anxiety. The SOM was rubbing his eyes in a way that seemed to indicate his disbelief. Emilia spoke into her handy and soon the gallery was being cleared.

The frisson of delight I had felt was collapsing into a state of apprehension as I edged my way towards the crowd. Raising myself on tiptoes, I managed a glimpse of the screen. The image was less than distinct, but it was clear enough that there was a structure. The structure was grained, as if somehow wooden. There was a blue, diffuse glow mingling with the orange of Titan's atmosphere. There was writing on the side.

'Put that up on the screen.' The SOM's voice was holding up, but barely. The structure filled the main view screen.

'Make it bigger, there, the writing.'

The controller zoomed in. In close, the structure looked even more wooden, even tree-like, but by now we were focussed on the words. A name. An English name.

***

Sascha gave me a gift, that night twelve years later. Well, it was actually two gifts. The first, the gift he intended to give, was some very interesting (and disturbing) papers in a battered old briefcase. The second, most precious gift that neither of us intended, was our daughter: Emilia Mary Rose.

***

Manhattan

Picture the scene: a hotel room. It has a bed in it, and curtains. The windows and the curtains are in front of you; they are closed, mostly, with a crack of an opening and a ray of sunlight timorously edging through. The bed is upended against the wall to the right of the door. The curtains are closed and you can't see the park but it's been there for fifty years and it doesn't really care if you can see it or not. There's a single dust mote, languorous in the beam.

Picture the scene: a writing desk of passable quality balances atop the perpendicular billet. One could imagine him writing at the desk, were the desk in a more accustomed position, say, in the middle of the room or adjacent to the window. The chair that once accompanied the adventurous desk lies splintered against the wall between the windows. A passable quality desk for 5th Avenue, perhaps: elegant, idiosyncratic, the pride and joy of a drawing room anywhere else.

Picture the scene: the middle of the room is empty of everything, including any carpet. Something has scorched and partly burned through the boards. Is that a wisp of smoke? The walls are decorated with a paper of fine filigree, at least at first glance. Upon closer inspection it's not paper but bare paint and Lichtenberg fractals. And there are scorch marks here too, almost like punctuation. The burn in the middle of the floor is circular, sort of, a little jagged, perhaps four feet in diameter.

He *was* here they say. Returned not long from triumph in Colorado. Triumph doesn't pay the bills. The picture makes no cause to differ. He was a mind like no other. Some say, in Colorado, he heard 'voices from another world "1… 2… 3…"' Of course, if you hold firm to twin axioms of the great man's enduring sanity and the persistent requirement for a rational explanation, then you arrive at Marconi, as many did and still do. But picture it, the scene.

There is a briefcase at your feet. There is writing on it – 'In settlement of my debts.' There is a shape on the briefcase, five-sided, crude. The writing is reddish, brown, rust-coloured. Still damp.

He *was* here, but no longer.

There are threads and pins and pictures. Not in the room but in my head. Colorado, pin. Pictures of lightning. Threads and pins back to the early days in Austria-Hungary, to Amboise and London, Edison, and Morgan and Long Island and that ridiculous tower. The tower that funnelled bolts of electrical energy into the ground. They didn't make it to the other side of the world, but they did make it to somewhere, to someone. Threads and pins. And pictures of lightning and, there in the corner of the laboratory, the shadow. The shadow in the lightning. The discolouration. The absence of something important. Maybe if you look at a sideways angle or glance at it quickly, before it gets chance to… Threads and pictures and pins. He woke them up.

Picture the scene. Or, alternatively, since the black and white still sits freely available now on the World Wide Web, don't. Hang the hat of your imagination upon the wall and google it: WA, Tesla, 5th Avenue. Do it soon, though, before they take it down. Four, oh four, imagination not found. It's been there for twelve years but they can't let it stay up now, not after Titan. They have too much to lose. Google or Bing it, don't picture it, don't take my word for it. After all, where has imagination ever gotten us?

***

The Chest in the Cellar

My Lord Essex, 1540 June 7th

Good tidings, my Lord. The transference is complete and the pressure is subsided sufficiently for me to sit and attempt to test this delightful imp. Such an endearing fellow he, all nuzzling affection. One could easily mistake his pendulous ears and expressive eyes for one of your hound pups, were it not for the perfectly formed yet tiny fingers with which he grips the stylus. I am watching as he scribbles the words I speak and think. My Lord, I must beg forgiveness if I cannot yet control my thoughts sufficiently to prevent his writing of my innermost missive. I shall suffer to be more disciplined in what is yet some hard exercise.

I make my report on this the first day of our journey in search of our heavenly Lord. All have behaved adequately and to our expectations. I go shortly to the wheelhouse and thence to attempt to commune with the Ndjinn. I shall provide further detail upon completion of the inspection. There, through the porthole aft, I see her rise! That beautiful orb, pearlescent she shimmers against the black. My Lord, 'tis such a sight as all should see! And there, pirouetting into view, blessed England, our pastures green and wooded hills!

I go, my Lord, in hope that from the churn you can take the words you need to be best informed. I shall attempt further when I have become more focussed.

Your servant, Wyatt

***

Thomas Wyatt, 1540 June 7th

Dearest Tom, think nothing of it. I agree with your assessment of our new companions. I am also ever in need of your verse; your absence, I fear, may lead to a fatal dearth of wit. Further, through your eyes, I see such sights as can only be dreamed of from our terrestrial confines. The King was here and sends his wishes for a safe voyage. It is a mite strange that the imp will not write while in his presence; she merely gazes at him all perplexed and he was forced to leave the chambers. The use of these beasts still gives him a foreboding. The ungodly are as tools for the betterment of England and the Faith but he must have results if his patronage and forbearance are to be maintained. May God protect you, Tom.

Essex

***

My Lord Essex, 1540 June 8th

I have completed my inspection of our Mary Rose; she goes well and our prospects look fair. At my request, the Bishop Bonner did not accompany myself and our chief Demoneer, your man Husee, upon our tour of the vessel. Why you insisted on sending this Bishop with us is far beyond me. He is ceaseless in his attempts at exorcism of myself, the crew, and the demon systema themselves. I have more than once reminded him that if the Almighty were to grant even one of his impassioned requests we should soon be without air or the ability to propel ourselves through the void or navigate. Yet he persists.

Our tour took us first to the wheelhouse, where I took a view through the forward glazing. The moon, ever larger, pours silver through the stained images of the virgin and our Lord and saviour. Helm guides us towards it. He is the strangest of the beasts that facilitate our endeavour, appearing as a complex set of spokes arranged as a wheel or a pentagram. Husee explains the workings of our systema in learnèd fashion. In my quiet moments I shall write a book: 'A Taxonomy of Demons and their uses for Spacefaering', or some such. It is a working title.

I should make a poem of it.

As Helm rotates about a central column, tendrils and nerves spread down the shaft into the body of the ship. They puncture the oaken skin, and the air shield, and expel tiny puffs of breath or flatus, I know not which, through tight sphincters into the space beyond. I am given to understand that this seeming small consequence is sufficient to adjust our heading and attitude with magnitude and accuracy.

Helm has three eyes on long stalks and a mouth that perches on a throat tube atop his central column. The mouth is near permanently configured into a most maniacal rictus, save every half of the hour or so when it booms 'I require SUSTENANCE!', upon which several rat-like creatures emerge, leaping from the forward mezzanine, and throw themselves into it [the mouth] with seeming joyous abandon. They sink quickly through his throat tube into a large fleshy sack at the base of the central column. In there, I assume, they are digested live and converted into the zephyrs that enable our guidance. I had started up the rope ladder to inspect the source of the rat-demons but Husee laid a hand on my shoulder and shook his head. By his account it would be improper to disturb the relentless copulation necessary to ensure the continued subsistence of the Helm.

From the wheelhouse we descended the second rope ladder – the first providing a route to the sleeping quarters – deep into the belly of the boat. We climbed through a hatch into a large hall space, the centre of which contained a golden tree, the trunk of which stood some hundred hands from the deck to before it gave over to myriad branches. The Lifegiver. As we descended to the deck I observed it more fully. I confess now that due to the accelerated pace of our venture, my time for familiarisation with my command before our commencement was unfortunately insufficient, and my preparation apparently inadequate. This was the first time I had laid eyes on our means of separation from the void and I was astounded by the beauty of it. Golden limbs and boughs sprayed out from the central trunk that rose straight and true, feeding branches and golden leaves that glittered and shimmered in the light from the Amberon swinging idly from the 'ceiling'. I have become easily accustomed to the notion of up and down provided to us by our Ndjinn; all of which would soon be replaced by the floating and associated bodily confusion preceding our slowing towards the moon.

We alighted upon the deck and Husee went immediately to the trunk. First he placed his hands against it and then leant his whole body in close to the golden bark. There was a rainbow ripple of colour that ran vertically through the bole. Knots in the wood contorted into what appeared to be a contented smile. I felt peace radiating from the pair. Husee beckoned to me that I should do the same and I tentatively made my way across the deck and mirrored Husee's deportment.

At first I felt a light tingling sensation pass through my mind and body, as if tiny threads were working through the spaces between the parts of me that were solid, led by gentle needles of purest kindness. Before long, the trickle became a stream, the stream a tributary that led to a river rushing headlong to an ocean. I knew the ocean was all of the heavens. All life was there and I could feel it, I was part of it, it was part of me. There were occasions with Bess when I had felt transcendent and free but never on this most tremendous of scales. The light and the darkness were exploded together as one and I felt myself falling into the depths and succour of salvation and liquid hope.

I felt Husee's hand on my shoulder and I woke unsurely. I do not know the time we had spent there but I noted that my legs were starting to drift away from the roots of the Lifegiver. We were floating, which I understood meant that we were changing attitude and preparing to slow. Husee explained that this was the perfect time to converse with the Ndjinn as he would be free of occupation for some time. From up the ladder I heard Helm singing in bawdy tone a modal tune of a different music with some wholly inexplicable words and terms.

'Yo HO boat's a floatin',
Yo HO gut's a bloatin',
Yo HO out it blurts and I convert,
Entropy into gravity.'

I felt the floor lurch beneath me and Husee and I were flung against the wall by the ladder, which was now the floor. A frown crossed the Lifegiver's trunk in knots and fissures. Helm laughed excessively. 'Entropeee into graviteee…' and then a sound of great relief and relaxation. I felt branches touch me and then wrap around my body, lifting me gently towards the tree. I did not resist and I was secure when Helm began another manoeuvre.

'Yo HO boat's a flippin',
Yo HO your gut's a trippin',
Yo HO and we're arse to front,
Inertia's such a vapid…'

I stopped listening at that point as I returned momentarily to the Lifegiver's reverie. After what seemed like only a few moments, I felt the branches relax. Floating next to me, Husee informed me that the more violent shifts were done and we should float to the Ndjinn's room.

Husee assured me that we could forego the ladders, so using one of the Livegiver's thicker limbs to steady ourselves we launched towards the far hatch. As we entered the corridor, Husee briefed me on the workings of the Lifegiver. Her limbs and roots are spread throughout the Mary Rose. To many perspectives she *is* the Mary Rose. She conveys our air throughout the boat, sensing where it may be depleted, cleaning it, and replenishing it. Where her branches permeate the outer skin they variously produce a kind of diffuse lightning shield that seals us from the void and grow more golden green leaves that take the light from the sun as food. Yet, of course, you know all this, my Lord, being chief in the planning of our venture. I think and speak now perhaps more for my own benefit than your own.

We emerged from the corridor into the Ndjinn's room. His excessive bulk was crammed in some sort of thin cloth chair with legs and arms of a strange light metallic substance. One side of the Ndjinn's room appeared to be open to the outside; I could see the moon so full that it filled a large proportion of the available area, as if the room had a moon-wall. It seemed to be getting larger by the second. I felt momentarily panicked, as if I would fall out and down to be dashed on the silvery expanse. I focussed on the chair; it was floating slightly.

The Ndjinn was the very vision of what a demon is *supposed* to look like; I imagine Bishop Bonner feels perfectly at home here. A life of ostensible chastity and propriety is justified all at once when confronted with this hellspawn made flesh. He is immense, muscular, and very red. Even so, the red colour was noticeably fading as we conducted our meeting. He has an angular, hideous face and small but pronounced horns that protrude viciously from each temple.

The Ndjinn had a plate of what could have passed for roasted pheasant – I could smell rosemary – were it not for the eight legs the 'bird' seemed to have. He ripped at a leg and offered it to me.

'Captain,' he boomed, 'try some. It is not unlike your English dog.'

My diplomatic sensibilities came to the fore – do not laugh when you read this, Cromwell – and I felt obliged to accept. I bit down and made an appreciative noise, although the taste was unusual.

'Excellent,' I commented. 'What is it?'

'Azarothian spider-turkey. Runt gets them.' He spoke through a mouthful of beast and gestured with his fork towards a miniature version of himself sat in the corner of the room disconsolately manipulating a glowing blue cube. As he moved his hands together and further apart the cube grew and shrank. At the Ndjinn's words, he seemed to come to life with a malicious grin. His voice was offensive to the ears, like a chorus of broken glass against slate.

'Would you like to see a live one?'

Before I could protest his eyes were full black and the cube was sparking with shafts of lightning. From the storm emerged an horrific beast, not spider, not bird, but some hideous chimera. Instinctively I threw my roast leg at it, which it captured in its mandible beak and devoured voraciously. It made as if to charge me but the Ndjinn waved his great red palm, from which emanated a bolt of light, turning the creature into a roast of similar exquisite quality to the former.

'Help yourselves, gentlemen.'

I was saved as an imp, similar to mine own, mounted in a wall recess, gave a small chirrup followed by an address to the room.

'Message from Helm is thus: "Fire it up, fucker."' Ndjinn gave a nod. We could hear booming laughter echoing down from the wheelhouse.

'On your word, Captain,' he addressed me.

I gave the order and Ndjinn sent his odd cloth chair floating to the Runt, who secured it. Strands of the Lifegiver emerged from the walls and wrapped themselves around the Ndjinn, securing him to the ship. The Ndjinn brought his hands together and formed what looked like a small billiard ball of brilliant blue light.

'This is called *Nuclear Fusion*,' he informed me.

He seemed to mould and shape the ball with his massive hands. As he did so, the ball grew larger and more orange, as a sun betwixt his empty palms. With an exaggerated flourish, he waved a hand over the top then pushed from behind. The front of the ball erupted, spewing a cast of lightning threads, woven together into a smooth glowing shaft that shot straight out of the room towards the burgeoning moon, which was now the absent floor of the room as I felt my weight returning to me. Were it not for a limb of the Lifegiver reaching out and supporting me, my earlier fantasy would have been realised! I clung to the tree limb gratefully as it laid Husee and me on the small ledge that runs around the voidspace. We made our way from the Ndjinn's room up the ladder, past the Lifegiver and Helm and then down to my sleeping quarters.

I can no longer see our home from my window and I must confess that I am beginning to feel the absence of England. Nevertheless, onward, my Lord. Onward.

Your servant, Wyatt

***

Thomas Wyatt, 1540 June 9th

Dearest Tom, thank you for your report. I have presented it to the King, who is today in dark spirits. I feel your news of good progress cheered him slightly but I am wary. I see him wracked by ambivalence regarding our venture. I am making preparations to secure the other demons, to protect against the eventuality that the King takes up against them. The Bishop too was at his behest; I am sorry that you are beset by his particular sort of piety and devotion. Trust you in Husee, as he will see you through if any man can. His efforts against the French under Lisle at Calais, and the knowledge he gained there, are the foundation of this endeavour.

When I am not reading your reports or writing through my imp she waits in the cellars at Austin Friars. She is locked away and protected with writing materials aplenty should your missives arrive in my absence. I keep our correspondence with her. I wrestle with choices for our next steps, but let not this be of immediate concern to you. Go with God's speed, Tom. May He protect us all.

Essex

***

My Lord Essex, 1540 June 10th

We have a problem. Bonner sits here in my quarters gibbering to himself; he has quite lost his wits. Husee tells me that there was an altercation, instigated by the delinquent bishop. Bonner attempted an exorcism on the Ndjinn's runt and it took umbrage. This offence became manifest in the form of thirteen lobster-like creatures, each walking upright on sandaled rear legs, no more than two hands tall, robed in rough cloth, waving their pincers about them as if deranged. One of them wore a crown of thorns; wherever it so wandered the others followed in some grotesque parody of our Lord and the Apostles.

Of course this incensed Bonner, who then proceeded to outdo himself. He renewed his attempts at exorcism with impassioned vigour. Only this time what he did or said must have actually realised some effect. The Ndjinn, the Runt, and even the wall-talk imp were suddenly wracked with pain, seemingly caused by bolts of lightning, the source of which we cannot fathom. We cannot converse with them and the Ndjinn's room is a dangerous place to venture, lest we become consumed by the lightning. Mercifully, the effect seems confined to that room; Lifegiver, Helm and others are unaffected.

I have tried to speak to Bonner but he is insensible. When he speaks any coherent utterance at all, it is in Latin.

Commend us to the King. Husee and I shall do all in our power to make this right. For England, my Lord.

Your servant, Wyatt

***

My Lord Essex, 1540 June 12th

Husee is dead. The moon recedes. We move away at ever greater speed. I become heavier. I have not heard from you in days, my Lord? All is well? Husee is dead, did I say this? I sent him to the Ndjinn's room to attempt to converse with the creature. Lightning struck him, is striking him. His body is blackened and crisp. I can glimpse it from the hatch. It turns to dust, I observe. The Ndjinn grows redder, he grows more pained, his lightning weave ever more intense. The pressure grows both figuratively and literally by the hour. We have been on too long, too long, too long. I do not know what to do, my Lord. I feel the weight.

Bonner is my only company now, save the imp, but he is silent. What has befallen you, my lord? Are you well? Bonner is company but no company. He speaks nothing if not in Latin. Over and over: 'A solis ortus cardine'. Sedulius, I think. The sun, I have seen the sun.

Our goddess moon, our Artemis,
to the hunt of the hind,
this fickle whip hath bloodied mine back,
this vain work my sorest lack,
and to whither hence, we cannot ken,
but to gold leaving her silver thus behind,
To England, my sweetest kiss.

There, my lord. It is not one of mine most auspicious, but it is what I have. Farewell to you and all we sought to do.

Yours always, Tom.

***

Amboise

They converse in French. It is the closest thing approximating a common language. The tall man with the magnificent moustache speaks poorly. The smaller man with the extravagant beard speaks fluently, if with a slight Italian accent.

They walk the grounds of the Château du Clos Lucé, alternating between conversation supported by vigorous gesticulation and quiet contemplation. One can clearly see they are two great minds in congress. They are trailed as they walk by a bald red dog. At a distance it is an ugly thing. Up close, it is an unspeakable atrocity, not a dog, but a stooped, red, stunted man-thing, with horns like a young goat. Come closer and you can hear them speaking.

'This is all very interesting, Nikola, but I am an old man. What do I care now for power and wealth?' Extravagant beard gestures to the grounds of the Château. 'Francis gives me everything I need.'

'Not power with politics. Power of *engine* or lightning. I show you. Runt show you.'

'Engine? Ingenium? Lightning? You speak in riddles. Were it not for the means of your arrival I think I would have Francis's men remove you for my own protection. You are Serbian, you say? I never met a Serbian who couldn't speak Italian; yet otherwise you do not seem so simple.'

'Yes, Serbian, also *American*. Across big sea and big time sea. Runt can open door.'

'American? More riddles for me to solve.'

They arrive at the lumber yard, where workmen are constructing a wooden machine. It has a central shaft with two circular wooden sails, perpendicular to the shaft.

'This machine,' Nikola gestures toward the construction, 'wants engine. I give you engine.' Nikola beckons to the stunted dogman-thing that he calls Runt.

'This is an Ornithopter. Francis wants to see it. I have told him that it will not fly and yet he insists that we try. He thinks it will finally see the English out of Calais! What is that thing doing?'

Runt has created a blue cube of lightning. There is a distinct smell of sulphur. The workmen put down their tools and all are watching. Some are kissing crucifixes or crossing themselves. From the lightning cube emerges a creature covered in some kind of viscous sludge. All are forced to retreat as the animal begins to shake itself free from the filth, flinging muck in all directions. Only Runt seems to enjoy being covered; he arches his hunched yet muscular back and breathes deeply of the coincident vapours.

Soon you see that the creature is not shaking but turning. It is an owl but not an owl. It has a fluff of feathers as an owl, but longer legs, which extend nearly a metre to the ground. It has a powerful-looking beak and seemingly unlimited turning, yaw, I guess, about the neck. Runt is holding what look like peanuts in a sackcloth bag. It feeds one to the owl and the head starts spinning again.

'Legume.' Runt speaks in English. His voice occurs simultaneously in three registers, the highest of which is a soprano shriek of damned souls, the lowest a bass that rumbles through the earth like the LA hyperloop from a souterrain apartment. The middle is an almost pleasant, yet somehow unspeakable, tenor that evokes memories of childhood torment. Think Bieber or Sheeran. 'Fuel for it. Now you give me my freedom.'

'Freedom? No beast. You will not have freedom yet. We have much work to do.' Nikola speaks confidently in English.

Runt gathers himself, and sparks of lightning start to build about his body, which glows scarlet in the evening half-light. His eyes turn blacker than coal. There is a growing sense that something murderous is about to occur. Then, with the air of one who has done this before, Nikola speaks some words in Latin. They are clumsily pronounced but nonetheless seem to have the necessary effect. The lightning consumes Runt and he howls in agony. This persists for a few minutes, before Nikola speaks again and the lightning subsides. Runt slumps. Owl's head stops spinning.

'Voila, Leonardo,' says Nikola Tesla, adjusting his collar and handing the bag of legumes to the bearded man, 'voici votre *moteur*.'

***

Pasadena

It is 2034. I was born fifty-two years earlier, in Darmstadt, Germany. My daughter Emilia is now sixteen years old. I finally left Darmstadt; we are now living in Pasadena. Emilia loves it of course; which sixteen-year-old girl does not love California? I still miss my home. Emilia is successful in school, very successful. More so than I was. She writes beautifully. I would be optimistic for her future, but I know what she is competing against.

Sascha was here a few weeks ago. He came for our birthdays. We see him only intermittently but a daughter's sixteenth birthday and her mother's fiftieth must be honoured, I suppose, even if it is over two years too late for the latter. Emilia does not seem to miss having a father, although she still wakes in the night. The Americans love their headshrinkers and the school recommended that she sees one. They say she draws pictures in class. She tells the teachers: 'This is Nikola Tesla, walking in the gardens with Leonardo da Vinci, and this is their demon who makes their magic animals.' I tell them she is just a creative girl but they shake their heads and tell me that she is suffering a trauma. I don't know, maybe she is.

We spoke, Sascha and I, about the briefcase and its contents. We spoke about Emilia and her dreams. Sascha tells me often how I have to help him in the fight. He sends me emails with links to news articles. I tell him I am a mother and I have a career, that we are safe. I do not really believe it. He tells me that I am the only person who can help.

Sascha is worried about Emilia's dreams. He told me about

his mother and growing up in Amboise. He told me about his travails in the early part of the last century, on the trail of Nikola Tesla, missing him in London in the cellar, missing him in Colorado, missing him in New York at the hotel. He thinks the dreams may be his fault. His mother was different, and so is he, you see.

I think I am weary now. This is disappointing because I am approaching a dénouement in my career. For the last fifteen years, seven in Darmstadt and eight in Pasadena, I have been working on the return to Titan. In fact, Huggie II (officially known as Sophia) touched down successfully only yesterday. I helped to make sure that she landed in the right place. This time there will be a drone, a tiny helicopter that I helped to design. It is going to look inside.

***

A few days after Sascha's visit I am at my station in the JPL control room. It is June 30th. After many system tests, Tycho has taken off successfully from Huggie II. It is flying through the atmosphere of Titan. I should be excited, apprehensive. I should be something. I am not. I am numb. The footage is being transmitted live around the planet. Soon everybody will know what I know.

A few hours and it is over and everybody in the control room is silent. They are unsure, unconvinced, even though they have seen it with their own eyes. I begin to pack up my things, when I feel a hand upon my shoulder. It is the chief, the mission controller.

'Can I speak with you, Dr. Schmidt?'

We go back to his office. He seats himself behind his desk and places his handy on the table. He is about to speak, when it beeps and, unbidden, Siri reads out a text message to him. It is short and over before he can cancel it.

'I'm sorry,' he says. He has a thick drawl, typical of those from the southern part of the United States. 'I asked you here because I want to explain something to you. Do you have a minute?'

I nodded. He indicates a chair in front of his desk. I sit.

'Firstly, I would like to thank you for your immense contribution to this project. I would go so far as to say that it could not have happened without you. I will be giving a press conference later today and I intend to mention you by name. Secondly, I noticed in the control room that you didn't react to the pictures we saw in the same way as the others.'

'Neither did you,' I respond. 'You do not seem phased or concerned at all.'

'Well, no. But then I knew what to expect.'

He sits up in his chair and a little forward. I watch as small protrusions form at the crest of each of his temples. His face becomes redder and more angular. He extends his arms and forms between his hands a ball of pure energy, contained in an iridescent sphere. I try to look surprised, but I do not have it in me. The ball of energy fades and disappears. The horns retract.

'I thought so,' he says. 'I will not ask you how you knew. But I do want you to know, we are not here to harm you and your people. We have been here for millions of years. We were in a long sleep but were awoken over a century ago, by the human measure of time.' He makes this last remark gently, without any trace of condescension.

'Some of us were used to enable that *Mary Rose* monstrosity, but they were only a misguided few. There were other follies too, dotted throughout history, most because of the brilliant idiot Serbian. We have power, a lot of power, but we do not intend to use it. Humankind will develop and grow at their own pace.'

'You are demons. How can we ever trust you?'

He smiles a little. 'Demons have always gotten a bad press. Do you believe in God? Don't answer, I know. If you don't believe in God then what are demons but different sapient species? I guess you could say we're from another dimension, but we ain't inherently evil; no more than humans are, anyhow. We've been living amongst you for over a hundred years. If we wanted to supplant or enslave you, wouldn't we have done it by now?'

A knock at the door, a head and a voice. 'You're needed on deck, chief.'

My Ndjinn boss nods, stands up. 'I'm sorry Anna. Here, take my number. If there's anything, anything at all that you want to ask me, don't hesitate.'

I sit for a moment. I have a thought. I suppress it because it is awful. As I am leaving, it creeps back and takes up residence. No matter what I do, where I try to direct my thoughts, it nags. It persists. It takes over.

***

Emilia and I land at JFK at 1745. We make our way to the transfer area and find seats. I take out my phone. I've prepared a text message, ready to send. I wonder how Siri will cope with the Latin.

There's a screen in the waiting area, showing BBC news footage of Tycho's feed. I watch it for the second time. The Mary Rose, Tycho finds a way inside. There are skeletons, human and… not human. Then there is the tree. The giant golden tree. There is Tom Wyatt, embracing the tree. He looks at peace and, unbelievably, like he is still alive.

I take out one of the papers from my laptop bag. I transferred them from the briefcase when it finally fell apart. Just as Tesla transferred them from the rotten cellar chest to the briefcase over one hundred years ago. Cromwell's chest. I read to myself, 'to whither hence… my sweetest kiss.'

My finger hovers over the send button as the TV screen

changes to show the chief giving his press conference. He can explain now, tell the world that there is nothing to fear. But there is. There is so much fear. Oh, Sascha. Sometimes I wish I had never met you. But then Emilia...

I press send. Seconds pass. The chief is at the lectern. He is suddenly afraid. Then he is glowing. Then there is nothing but brilliant white. Then static.

***

We are on the plane to Frankfurt. The sun is setting, filling the cabin with an orange glow. Sunrise, sunset. There is a new sun in Pasadena, but short-lived. A solis ortus cardine. From lands that see the sun arise. A new dawn will come tomorrow, not for me but for Emilia. My Emilia Mary Rose. Dream your beautiful dreams in hope and expectation. Dream your powerful dreams forever free of demons. Dream your dreams in Darmstadt. At home, where it all began.

The Devil's Tongue

By JES Simpson

Nicholas sat in the hallway of his master's home, waiting. The only servant he had seen was the young boy who had opened the door to him and bid him sit on the chair while he fetched the master.

Waiting idly, he examined the condition of his blue hose, white tunic, and black coat, rubbing the coarse material between his fingers. He then fiddled slightly with the modest ruff around his neck. At his feet, a canvas bag contained a change of clothes and some reading material. His instructions had said to prepare for a short trip.

Stomach grumbling, Nicholas glanced down the hallway, hoping to see the boy and maybe get something more substantial than the stale bread he'd wolfed down for breakfast. As his gut growled again, he got up from his chair, placed his bag against the wall and made his way to the laboratory to see if he might ascertain what was detaining his master.

Entering the chamber, he breathed in the heavy smell of chemicals, chalk, and dust. Bookcases and shelving lined most of the walls, cluttered with various astrological and alchemical devices as well as a healthy collection of books. In the centre of the room, a large table, similarly cluttered, dominated the space.

The remaining wall sported a collection of large slates covered in various mathematical formulae and odd symbols which had been collected by the room's only occupant. In his early sixties, with a scholarly cap covering his grey hair, Dr John Dee wore his usual black robes, which were stained with chalk and had clearly seen better days.

Nicholas coughed pointedly and the old man turned and focused his attention on him, his dark brown eyes shining with excitement and a keen intelligence, then smiled affectionately.

'Hah, Nicholas, my boy! I think I'm onto something here. It's a little crude but it definitely lends itself to my theories, and maybe more.'

He turned, gesturing excitedly at some of the strange symbols scrawled on the slates. Nicholas looked closely at some of the scribblings on the board. He had to admit it was over his head, but then if he understood everything, he wouldn't be the assistant.

'Dr Dee, you had a task for me. I've been waiting for you in the hall,' he said, trying to keep the annoyance from his voice.

'Hmm? Oh, yes, yes. Apparently, there's a demonic possession in Margate. I'd like you to observe. Your notes are always so thorough. I need to know what is said. Language is of utmost importance to understanding, yes?' He pulled his focus reluctantly from the slates and looked Nicholas up and down. 'I have requested a carriage for you.' Dee glanced at the light coming in through one of the high windows of the room. 'Which should be here by now.'

He waved Nicholas out of the room and towards the front door.

The carriage was indeed waiting already. Dee ushered him out to it, allowing him scant time to pick up his bag on the way.

'It shouldn't be a long journey and the clergy are already involved, so be careful. I want every detail of what is said by the subject. Safe journey, my boy!'

With that, the elderly scholar was already walking back

into his home, his right hand still clutching a piece of chalk, distractedly sketching symbols in the air.

***

Seated comfortably within the carriage, as it wound its way through London's streets, Nicholas resigned himself to reading to pass the time but, book in hand, he found it hard to stay focused.

He pondered the sciences, evolving as they were, the way their understanding of the universe itself was growing. The church was doing all it could to quell the surge in general interest. It frustrated Nicholas, a devout Christian. He reached up to his chest: beneath his tunic, a simple silver cross, a gift from his mother, reminded him of his faith. Surely at some point there would be a unification of science and faith. One should not be exclusive of the other.

Dr Dee has regularly discussed this, often late into the night. A lot of Dee's research deals with old languages. He says he can navigate the future by understanding the past. Those old texts of his are religious tomes and scientific papers. He flits between the two with ease, so why can't society be the same? Accepting of faith but understanding of science?

While he pondered the implications, the carriage slowed down. Knowing that they had barely left the London boroughs, Nicholas glanced out through the rain.

They were approaching a large, well kept, house. Nicholas could not help but stare as a very attractive young lady approached the carriage. Behind her, a stoic looking man of some years carried a bag, which he passed to the driver as the young lady waited for someone to open the carriage door.

Feeling every bit the bumbling fool, and wiping rain from his face, Nicholas opened the door and stepped out.

'Madam, if you would?' he invited, gesturing into the

carriage. 'To hesitate in this ungodly weather is to be soaked to the skin.'

She smiled disarmingly and blushed slightly as she stepped past him, an aroma of rose blossoms in her wake. Seeing the book on Nicholas's bench, she made herself comfortable on the opposite side.

Returning to his seat, he smiled at the young lady, taking her in. Curly red hair framed a pale delicate face, deep hazel eyes had a flash of amber to them, and the blush on her cheeks, matching the faint colour of her lips, only accentuated her beauty. Fashionably attired, and properly so, her blue and white dress and bodice did little to hide her figure, and Nicholas berated himself for a momentary lapse into improper thoughts.

'May I introduce myself, Miss, as there is no one here to make introductions? I am Nicholas Whitehall, a student of the sciences and assistant to the Queen's Special Advisor, Dr John Dee.' He puffed his chest out in the hope that his title, albeit slight, would still impress.

'It is a pleasure to make your acquaintance, Mr Whitehall. I am Elsbeth Jones, on my way to visit Margate for a day or two to get some fresh sea air.' She leaned forward conspiratorially. 'I find staying in the city for too long makes me restless.' She offered him the sweetest smile Nicholas had ever seen.

***

The journey flew by. Elsbeth was attentive and curious, asking all manner of questions about his work with Dr Dee and his own personal preferences for study. And it was with a heavy heart that Nicholas parted from her in the late afternoon, once they had arrived in Margate..

Helping her down out of the carriage, Nicholas kissed the back of her hand, which was surprisingly cold.

'I do hope to see you again, Mr Whitehall,' she said, offering a perfect curtesy, before making her way off up the hill, a local boy in tow carrying her bag.

The driver coughed pointedly and handed Nicholas his own bag, gesturing down the hill.

'Nearest inn's the Lion's Share, just down that way, sir. Should be able to secure yourself some lodging with ease.'

Thankful for the directions, he handed over a penny. The driver nodded and mounted the carriage, steering it away back up the hill.

As he made his way in the direction of the inn, he breathed in the deep crisp, salty air and admired the coastal view. An occasional ship could be seen making its way from out on the dark foreboding sea. A storm on the horizon was moving in, and the sun, slowly setting behind him, seemed to do little to ward off the approaching gloom.

***

Nicholas approached the bar in the Lions' Share inn, he banged his hand down twice and called out to a doorway that possibly led to the kitchen.

'Service, please,' he said loudly, and, within a few moments, an old lady appeared. Her apron was stained, but she carried herself proudly as she stepped towards the bar and eyed Nicholas with bright blue eyes that belied her apparent age.

'Evening, sir. What can I be helping you with? We carry a fine ale, but the evening meal won't be ready for about an hour.' She smiled and absentmindedly wiped the bar with the corner of her apron.

'Good lady, I require lodgings for the night, maybe two. I'm on business of the Queen's court.'

Pursing her lips in thought, she turned to stick her head into the kitchen. 'Harold, go make sure the lodgings are swept and clean.' Turning back to Nicholas, she smiled apologetically.

'It's a penny a night and a penny for two days' meals. If you don't mind taking a seat while the room is swept? We haven't had a lodging in a week or two. Most tend t' lodge down the coast near the harbour.' She gestured towards a table on one side of the common room.

'That will be fine, madam. It was a long journey from London, an ale will do nicely while you're about it.'

Picking up his bag he placed it next to the unoccupied table and proceeded to make himself comfortable, while the landlady poured an ale and carried it over. As she placed the mug on the table Nicholas handed her four pennies.

'I may be keeping some odd hours and would appreciate it if food could be made available as and when,' he said as she deftly pocketed the coins.

She smiled and nodded, then, with a curious look, sniffed the air.

'Thas' fine, young master, but I must tend the evening meal, or it'll burn. The young un, isn't in there tending it. If you need anything, just call.' And she hastily retreated into the kitchen.

While he waited, and drank his ale, a steady flow of customers made their way into the inn. Every time the door opened the storm outside could be heard getting closer. The landlady appeared often to serve customers and light candles, and, as Nicholas reached the end of his ale, a sullen young boy, about twelve years of age, walked quickly through the common room, broom in hand, as he made his way into the kitchen. A few minutes later he was back to shutter the windows against the coming storm. The landlady soon appeared in front of Nicholas's table with a plate of cooked meats, fish, and boiled vegetables. Nicholas had forgotten exactly how hungry he was. He thanked her and started eating, savouring the simple but satisfying fare.

As he finished eating, Nicholas took the time to examine the young boy, who was now tending the fire in the common room. He looked upset, like he had been crying recently.

Nicholas wasn't the only one watching the boy: some of the locals were talking amongst themselves and glancing over every now and then. Occasionally, one of them would make the sign of the cross, with expressions of either fear or pity on their faces.

Nicholas called to the boy, asking for another ale and, when he returned with it, he gestured at the spare seat at his table.

'What is your name, boy?'

The boy, still standing, looked around the inn, but the landlady was nowhere to be seen.

'Harold, sir. Sorry, but I 'ave chores to be tending to,' he replied, his rough-cut brown hair across his face as he lowered his shoulders in a half bow, his pale blue eyes red raw and his cheeks equally flushed.

'May I ask what has you out of sorts, Harold?'

The boy glanced around again, clearly uncomfortable talking to this stranger. 'I'm not to talk of it, sir. It'll bring evil spirits to the household.'

Nicholas smiled in what he hoped was a disarming manner. 'Is it about the boy under the church's care?'

'Aye sir. A friend o' mine. He did naught to attract the devil's ire.' He touched his brow and shoulders in the form of a cross and glanced around nervously. This time the landlady was back, and, seeing the interaction, she had started walking over to the table.

'Harold, get yourself back in the kitchen, lad. Don't pester the young master.' she said tersely.

'Madam, would it bother you if I asked Harold here a couple of questions about his friend?' Seeing the worried look on her face, he added: 'Nothing that would draw undue attention to yourselves, I assure you.' A little too late, Nicholas noticed that a lot of the inn's customers were already paying heed to the conversation.

'If it's the Queen's business, who am I to say no?' the landlady answered, a little louder than necessary. 'But mind your words, Harold.' She patted the boy's shoulder affectionately, protectively, and then looked Nicholas in the eye. 'Pardon me for saying, sir, but I'll have no ill spirits drawn into these godly premises, so please mind your words too.' She glanced around at the patrons in her inn, making eye contact with those that were observing them and then made her way towards the kitchen. 'And not too long, as he has chores!' she called over her shoulder as she disappeared through the doorway.

Nicholas looked at the boy and gestured to the chair.

'So, what is the name of the boy who was taken ill?' he asked quietly as Harold reluctantly sat down opposite him.

'Matthew, sir. We been friends since forever.'

"And did you see him fall ill?'

'Possessed, they say, by a demon or something,' Harold mumbled as he shook his head.

'Yes, well, did you see him before he was taken by the clergy? Do you know what happened?' Nicholas asked, taking a sip of his ale.

'I know his da is right angry with him. Said he was always a curse, due to Matthew being slow and all. Most folk think he's dumb, but he's not, just a bit slower is all.'

Nicholas pressed on. 'Do you know what happened? What was he like before they took him?'

'Aye, they were out fishing. His da said he'd hit his head and fell in the drink. He'd had to dive in for him. Lucky they made it back at all. But Matthew, when they woke him, back on the beach, he couldn't speak right, like he was talking foreign or something.'

'So, he awoke speaking a different language?' Nicholas asked, trying not to sound too eager.

'Aye, sir, but nothing like I've heard, not like French or anything.' The boy fidgeted and looked to where the landlady was serving another patron the evening meal.

'Thank you, Harold. That's a great help. You can go now. If you think of anything else please let me know?' Nicholas smiled.

Harold stood and nodded. 'I will, sir. Thank you.' He walked off into the kitchen, where soon afterwards the sound of pots and pans being scrubbed could be heard.

Nicholas drank his ale as the growing storm wailed outside, as if banshees surrounded the inn. By the time he'd finished his third ale, the common room was about empty, and, as he watched the locals brave the storm, he became acutely aware of exactly how exhausted he was.

***

As he retired to his room Nicholas's head swam. Kneeling before his cot, the wind and rain battering the shutters, images of the upset Harold were replaced by recollections of his journey with Elsbeth, and then nightmarish images of a boy laid on a beach. While the shutters groaned, the storm raging on, Nicholas tried to shake his head free of the troubling images and thoughts. Seeking the solace of his faith, he prayed.

'Dear Lord, I ask you to lend me courage and the strength to face what may come, to stand up to ignorance, where I can. Help me to see the truth of what lies before me.

***

After a very poor night's sleep, Nicholas was all but relieved to leave his pallet, dress himself, and set out early from the inn. The weather was now the complete opposite of the night before, with the sun shining down brightly on the recently battered coastline.

He walked the main route towards the church. It was an impressive thoroughfare, small compared to London, to be sure, but considerable for the size of this community, growing though it was. Reaching the main doors, which were large oaken affairs with heavy iron work, he knocked on them diffidently as he entered. The building's interior was pleasant and showed off a certain wealth.

'Hello?' he called.

Shortly after, a male voice replied from the direction of what must be the vestry. 'Over here, my son. I'm afraid we are a bit busy. Unless it is of utmost urgency, could you come back another time?' A middle-aged man, dressed in priestly robes, with a gaunt face and balding head, followed the voice out.

'Alas, father, I wish that I could. I have been sent by the Queen's court to document the incident with the boy.'

The priest stepped further into the hall. 'Well, I can't say that I see the need. The church has this well in hand.' Despite his words, something about his demeanour appeared relieved.

'As that should be, father, but my master is the Queen's most trusted advisor and, thusly, we have Her authority in this matter. I shall endeavour not to obstruct you in your duties in any way.'

Holding his hands out in front of him the priest bowed his head, while keeping his tired brown eyes on Nicholas. 'Be warned, my son. Exorcism is not for the faint of heart.'

Nicholas nodded. 'I have witnessed a few now, at the behest of my master, and I am well aware that they can be a harrowing experience for all concerned.'

The priest smiled, his relief entirely apparent now. 'I am Father Jacobs. This is my church, but Father Tildow is overseeing the exorcism. He has had a lot more experience than myself, although I will confide to you that his methods are somewhat unusual. He is the only member of the local clergy ordained for exorcism.'

Nicholas returned the smile. 'Nicholas Whitehall. I would say it's a pleasure to be here, Father Jacobs, but the circumstances could be happier.'

They shook hands. Then Father Jacobs gestured for Nicholas to follow him back through the church. Passing through a door, they travelled down a short corridor and entered a small annex.

'I find this whole situation quite distressing. Matthew was such a sweet boy. His family have been attending this church for generations.'

'I heard the father was unhappy with having a simpleton for a son?' Nicholas suggested.

Father Jacobs stopped abruptly and turned to face him. He spoke in sharp but hushed tones: 'Kenneth is many things, and I will not sully my tongue with such gossip, but he is a God-fearing man and would never harm his boy. Matthew was a typical, if not bright, boy. I would beg you, therefore, to keep all other speculation to yourself, as the family are distraught enough.'

Nicholas stepped back from the priest with a nod. 'I meant no disrespect; I just need to document as much as I can about the situation.'

Father Jacobs moved towards a door at the end of the annex.

'I will advise Father Tildow of your presence. Please, wait here.'

The priest left the room, closing the far door behind him, but not before foul vapours from the room beyond had assailed Nicholas. He gagged on sea water, human waste, incense, and something else that he couldn't put his finger on. He could only imagine the sort of unholy corruption that might cause such a stench.

Indistinct voices rose from behind the door and, not long after, Father Jacobs reappeared, along with another noxious assault.

'Father Tildow is conducting the hourly rite. If we wait a short while he will take a reprieve, and it will be safer for you to enter. Come, I will show you where you can wait.'

They went back through the church to another annex, which, with a kitchen to one side, apparently served as a small dining area. A door in the south wall was open and led out to a garden.

'I could do with some air. Would you mind if we sat in the garden?' Father Jacobs asked politely, as Nicholas gestured him on.

'You must tread this path carefully, Nicholas,' Father Jacobs said softly as they approached a pair of damp stone benches in the simple but well-sheltered garden. The natural scent of damp earth, herbs, and other aromatic plants gave them a reprieve from what they had just been breathing.

'Father Tildow is a member of an older order. Just your talk of wanting to understand the demonic could lead him to suspect you already cavort with the damned. I wouldn't normally say any of this about another man of the cloth, of course, but he unsettles me, and his methods… well.' Leaning back on the bench, the priest looked back though the doorway to be sure they were not about to be overheard. 'You say you have witnessed other exorcisms. Were you convinced of evil's touch in every case?'

Nicholas was somewhat taken aback by the confidences so freely being shared by the priest. 'Out of the three I have previously documented, only one of them, I would say without a doubt, could only be explained by demonic maleficence. The others could have been explained more mundanely if I'd had the opportunity to investigate further.'

Father Jacobs smiled uncomfortably. 'As a younger man I had a leaning towards the sciences, but the good Lord had other plans for me. I suspect we will need more men of your inclination in years to come, Nicholas.'

Nicholas decided he quite liked Father Jacobs, as he was refreshingly open-minded for a man of the cloth. They sat in comfortable silence and contemplation for some time, Father Jacobs checking the doorway periodically.

'Father Tildow should be finishing this hour's rite.' The priest stood, smoothed out his robes, and leaned in towards Nicholas. 'Please keep my views between us? I do not need to remind you, I'm sure, that there are those in both the church and the court who would see us prosecuted for heresy otherwise.'

Nicholas nodded in agreement as they rose together and walked back into the church. When he had taken on his role as Dr Dee's assistant, he had been similarly warned, by Dee himself, often in little asides, as the doctor bemoaned how orthodoxy, fools and 'stagnant minds' constantly sought to kick the stool out from under progress, to hang them all with ignorance.

As they approached the door back into the church, Nicholas was abruptly forced to step backwards, as a hulking figure of a man shouldered his way through.

'Father Jacobs,' boomed Father Tildow, 'I would have an ale and something to eat. I fear this day is but beginning and the Lord's work is far from over.'

The giant was in begrimed, brown robes, and reeked of ash and the odd smell from before, which Nicholas now recognised as sulphur.

Father Jacobs hastily ducked into the kitchen area and brought out bread, meats, and cheeses, along with a large mug of ale, for the dining table, as Nicholas backed further away from the imposing Father Tildow.

Wiping sweat from his mighty bald pate on his robes, the large priest finally turned his intense gaze on Nicholas. The priest held up a single finger, forcing Nicholas to wait while he was examined. After what must have been close to a minute, Nicholas could stand the scrutiny no more, bowed and introduced himself.

'Father Tildow, I presume. I am Nicholas Whitehall, assistant to Dr John Dee, the Queen's Advisor.'

Father Tildow took a seat at the table and a large swill of ale before responding. 'I have no time for scholars of your ilk, sir, and your Dee is a heretic. Yet I smell no taint on you. Hinder me not in God's work and I will accede to your presence.' His voice filled the space. He raised a fist the size of a boulder and brought it crashing down on the table. Ale sloshed and food stuffs scattered from plates. 'Mark me, though. Interfere, and I shall be your undoing. I shall bring such ruination upon you, that none would ever recognise you as a man made of God again. You are a man of God, are you not?'

'Y-y-yes, sir, I am a man of God.' And to prove it, he hastily showed the silver cross beneath his tunic. 'Your threats are unnecessary, sir. My task here is not to hinder, but to observe, and learn.'

Father Jacobs, placing yet another platter of food stuffs before Tildow, took Nicholas by the elbow and began to guide him out into the hallway. 'Seeing as time is in short supply, why don't we see to your observations, Nicholas?'

Only too happy to be escaping out from under the giant priest's baleful gaze, Nicholas allowed Father Jacobs to lead him once more. Instead, let the cheese suffer the priest's terrible inspection and dire threats as if it was the very devil itself.

***

As they made their way towards the chamber containing the boy Matthew, Father Jacobs cast occasional anxious glances back at Nicholas. At the door, the priest hesitated, with his hand on the handle.

'You must know, Nicholas, this is not to my liking. The way Father Tildow casts out foul spirits and demons is… unorthodox. It galls me to talk so of his methods, for he is a man of God.'

Nicholas nodded in mute understanding. Father Jacobs took a deep breath, pushed the door wide and they entered.

All but immediately Nicholas was overwhelmed by an unholy stench and an oppressive heat. The single chamber had little to no natural light, with the windows shuttered tight, and a brazier in each corner of the room burning sickly sweet incense. Smoke filled the air, threatening to choke them. The only other furniture in the cell was a cot, in the centre, and a lectern before it, upon which sat a large, open tome.

A young boy was prone on the cot, his hands and feet lashed to the corner posts. He was naked except for a cloth tied around his midsection. He had soiled himself and that, combined with the incense, had Nicholas's stomach churning.

Buckets of sea water were placed tactically around the room, and switches made of willow or birch were leant against the walls. Bible verse had been scrawled in chalk on the walls, alongside the name of the archangel Michael, repeated numerous times.

Nicholas hesitantly stepped forward, his senses reeling. The boy groaned and tried to speak, but he was gagged.

'What torture is this Father Jacob?' Nicholas asked in horror.

'He was found to be speaking in the Devil's tongue, the language of demons and evil spirits. The gag is to prevent that foulness from poisoning others. Father Tildow seeks to purify the body, to free his soul of the corruption.'

Nicholas hissed though his teeth. There were lashes on the boys back, sore, angry looking welts. Drenched and shivering, Matthew barely seemed aware of Nicholas's presence. On the side of his head a dark reddish white ichor seeped from a deep cut. It had to be the injury from the fishing accident. It had clearly gone untreated and was now infected.

Forcing himself to think objectively, and wiping a tear from his eye, Nicholas glanced over to the priest.

'Father Jacobs, I need to hear him. I will remove the gag, just for a moment. It is the reason I have come to this place. I assure you I will waste no time replacing it afterwards.'

The priest positioned himself on the other side of the cot, hands clutching the wooden crucifix that hung around his neck.

'If you must. I will safeguard you, but be quick, or Matthew will not be the only one getting a lashing from Father Tildow.'

Nicholas knelt in front of the thin boy, whose eyes were unfocused and rolling. His skin was entirely pale, but burned to the touch as Nicholas pulled down the gag.

'Matthew, my name is Nicholas. Please, can you tell me what ails you?'

Matthew's eyes found him with a confused and teary appeal. The boy coughed and swallowed, working to moisten his mouth. The braziers crackled in the corners of the room as Matthew, now looking around in fear, stretched his jaw, swallowed again and rasped: 'Ig barb lout harat hinf bundler mondro. Ig lout haraund junta!'

Nicholas blinked. There was no malice in these words. The boy was pleading, and pained, but speaking gibberish.

'I'm sorry, Matthew. I don't understand you. What language are you speaking?'

'Ig ranut barb, hanak muntro jint.'

The boy began to weep, wracking sobs pulling at Nicholas's heart. He looked in appeal at Father Jacob, who reluctantly placed the gag back in the boy's mouth. Matthew had no strength left to struggle.

'This?' Nicholas asked sternly as he stood, pointing down at the boy. 'This is your Devil's tongue?'

Father Jacob cast his eyes down in shame. 'Father Tildow has named it so, and it is my duty to assist him. He is the local church's authority on the matter.'

They stood in silence for a moment, the only sound that of the boy whimpering. Nicholas stared at Father Jacobs in disgust. His fists clenched. The anger within him meant he hardly trusted himself to speak.

The door to the chamber suddenly swung open and Father Tildow walked in, food and ale now added to the filth of his robes. He addressed Nicholas, apparently oblivious to the mood in the room: 'It is time for another reading of the rite. You may stand witness. Father Jacobs, more blessed sea water.'

Father Jacobs bowed his head in assent and collected some empty buckets from near the door. 'I will see to it now, Father Tildow,' he muttered, stepping out behind Tildow's spreading shadow.

'Now, sir, you should stand against the wall and remain silent. Do not interfere, or I will be forced to act with a sudden brutality in the way of the blessed archangel Michael.' As he spoke, he fiercely grasped the silver cross round his neck in a huge meaty fist. Nicholas found himself obeying the priest, backing up against the sooty wall.

Father Tildow stepped to the lectern, placed one hand on the open pages and, without glancing down, proceeded to chant the exorcism rite: 'Exorcizamus te, omnis immundus satanica potestas, omnis incursio infernalis adversarii!'

Still reciting the words, he now lifted his hand from the book and paced around the cot. He took up a switch, dipped the end in the salt water, and then whipped himself on the back twice, fast, before returning it to the water. And then whipped Matthew once with it. The boy screamed into the gag, and convulsed.

Nicholas flinched with every stroke, appalled by what he was witnessing, his stomach in knots.

'I am the right hand of the archangel Michael! With his blessing do I cast you out! With the power of the Almighty I cast you out! Your hold cannot endure, demon. You shall submit to God's will through me.' There was a rising zeal in Father Tildow's voice, as he whipped himself again, and then struck the boy a second time.

Nicholas stared at the monstrous priest, in his sodden, ash smeared robes. Father Tildow threw the switch aside and placed his hand back on the book, his words sounding feverish and maniacal now. Was that a smile on his lips? Was he enjoying this?

He desperately wanted to intervene, to end the boy's suffering, but he found he could not. Finally, unable to watch another moment, Nicholas turned away. 'I have seen more than enough!' He fled the room.

Nicholas ran from the church, nearly falling over Father Jacobs on the way, as the priest struggled with two buckets.

'Nicholas! Wait!'

'I have all I need, Father. Believe me, this will be fully documented and reported. I must make the next carriage back to London! Goodbye!'

***

A lurch of the carriage awoke him from his slumber, and he was delighted to discover he had been joined by his comely former companion.

'Miss Elsbeth! What a pleasure! But whatever must you think of me? Why did you not wake me?'

'You seemed very much in need of the sleep, Mr Whitehall. Sleep does so restore one's spirits, no?' she replied with a twinkle.

'Quite so, Miss Elsbeth,' he warmed. 'I must confess that of late I've had something of a harrowing ordeal.' And he told her of all that had occurred.

'Oh, that poor soul!' she exclaimed. 'How beastly this Father Tildow sounds. He should be the one tied up and switched!' In her agitation, she had crossed the carriage, sat next to him, and placed her hand on his knee. 'And you had insufficient opportunity to study the language of the demon?'

'Alas that is so,' he sighed, placing his hand on hers, marvelling at how cool it was.

At that moment, the temperature in the carriage seemed to be plummeting, and the reek of sulphur was all around. As he turned to look at Elsbeth he turned to ice.

Her smile was a rictus grin, drool stringing down her chin, her eyes rolled up into her head, with only the whites were showing.

He was paralysed with fear, even breathing difficult. Elsbeth slowly rose and placed a hand on Nicholas's shoulder pushing him down until he was lying on the bench.

'Oh, dear, dear, Nicholas. We can't have you going back to Dee with nothing to show for your hard work, now can we?'

Her voice distorted, as if many voices were speaking at once. He felt a cold sweat and trembled. He was powerless to do anything but stare up at her demonic visage.

'We have a little message for your doctor, just a little something. If it was up to this one alone, she would have her fun with you, but we have been told not to harm you too much, and she does like you so.' She giggled childishly one moment, and seductively the next.

'Now, how to convey our help to your Doctor Dee?'

At the mention of the Doctor's name a chorus of distorted sounds built into a crescendo within her voice, the sound of ice cracking, the clink of chains against a dungeon wall, the hiss of freshly heated steel plunged into cold water.

Nicholas's senses were stretched to their limit.

'He is so close to the right path, so close to understanding, that it would be a shame not to give him a nudge. We are *inspiration* after all.'

The air rippled with energy, smelling like a lightning storm. It overpowered him and he felt his sanity and consciousness slipping away. She produced a delicate, curved blade from under her bodice, and licked it, blood trickling from the corner of her mouth. She whimpered in ecstasy. It took everything he had just to close his eyes, to fight off the nightmare before him.

'Yes, close your eyes, dear, sweet, Nicholas. You need not be awake for this,' she whispered at his ear, as she unbuttoned his jacket, and lifted his tunic.

'Ah yes, there's our canvas.'

***

Nicholas came awake as the carriage pulled up outside Doctor Dee's residence. He groped for his bag. The journey here was foggy in his recollection. He climbed out of the carriage and looked up at Doctor Dee's home. It was only then he noticed a bloody pattern seeping through his tunic.

Solomon's Prime Key

By Nozomi Okumura

'Oh, for–… Grant?'

He could hear the frustration in Mark's voice. He sighed, leaning forward from his slouch. 'What?'

'How's your internet?'

'It's–' He checked his phone. Tap. Tap. 'Yep. Gone.'

'How many times…'

'Check the router.'

'Nah, man, just talk to him. That's what we're paying for.'

Grant frowned. He pulled at his face, which felt older every time he did it. 'Whose turn is it?'

'Uh…' Grant heard Mark poking around in the corridor adjacent to the lounge. The clack of wood on wood tipped him off to what he was doing. 'Yours.'

'You just flipped the sign.'

'Does it matter? Just do it, man. It's no big deal.'

'You're standing right there!'

'No, I'm not!' Mark shouted, from slightly further away.

'Dude!'

'Can't hear you! What?' This time Mark shouted, coupled with a laugh, from the stairs. Grant cursed, standing up from the couch and stretching out from the last four hours of reading. He headed into the corridor and turned to the door immediately on his right. The reversible sign hanging from the nail had been knocked askew by Mark's haste to turn it to the side that read, in printed floral text, *'The trash needs putting out'*. He scowled, turning it back over so it read *'The recycling needs putting out'*, and knocked on the door.

'Enter,' croaked the voice from inside. Grant rolled his eyes, gripping the warm metal handle and pushing his way into the room. A wall of sulphurous stench greeted him – three months ago, he may have gagged, but now he simply wafted his hand before his nose and cleared his throat.

A thick smoke filled the large room, rendering its occupant almost invisible. The more Grant tried to clear the air, the thicker it swarmed around him. He squinted, bringing the almost-human mass in the far corner into focus, along with the tiny speck of light that illuminated it. 'You're smoking again, Mal,' Grant stated. The words invited the smoke into his mouth, and caused him to gag. 'C'mon, man. Uncool.'

'Hm?' The voice was right at Grant's ear, suddenly filling his mind, to the very darkest corners. Not a voice – it was the crippling song of some perverse creature that had linked their minds in order to communicate. 'Oh. Sorry. One sec–'

A deep, ragged sucking noise filled the room. Slowly, the smog rolled back and retreated, like roots shrivelling in sunlight, returning to the beak of the creature from which it had first spewed. Two wings, each larger than Grant's body by half, unfurled and stretched, scraping against the walls and ceiling. Attached to them, a black-feathered body straightened from its hunch and displayed the beaked, round head with wide, bulbous brown eyes. The creature tipped its head slightly to one side, to fix on Grant. 'Better?' it rumbled.

'Better.'

'What's up?' the creature – Mal – set the light down, revealed to be his mobile. It drew Grant's eye for a moment, and he saw a video paused on the screen.

'Internet's broken.'

'Is it?' Mal looked down, stooping like an old man with poor hearing, his head to one side as he examined his phone. 'Mine's fine.'

'You on data?'

'Oh. Yeah.'

'You mind taking a look?'

Mal reached up to his face with long, spindly arms and gave the tuft of black around his face a scratch, not unlike Grant did when he let his stubble grow out. 'Have you turned it off and on again?'

'Mark must have by now,' Grant lied.

'Uh-huh.' Mal sighed, a tiny tongue of smoke escaping from his beak.

'You alright?'

'Yeah, just – yeah. Yeah, I'm good.'

Grant paused. Frowned. Part of him didn't want to ask, but the dejection in Mal's voice scraped differently against the inside of his skull. Mal was usually full of rasping cheer. 'I've known you long enough to know when you're covering something up.' Mal didn't answer – his beak just clicked softly. 'Come on, man. You can talk to me. What's going on?'

Another, heavier sigh. This one saw black smog gouting from Mal's beak, a darkness that twisted and sparked as if flint were being struck. It pooled on the floor between them, swirling ominously. So long as it remained there, Grant wasn't about to mention it. 'Three-hundred and seventy-three.'

'Huh?'

'That's the number of years between now and my first ever summoning.'

'No way.'

'Yes way,' Mal huffed, loosing another spurt of smog. 'Three-hundred and seventy-three years ago, I was summoned to the realm of a minor lord. He wished for me to win him the adoration of the innkeep's daughter, sparing him the shame of having to stoop so low as to do it himself.'

'Did you?'

'I told him what I told you the last four times you've asked me to look at the internet.' Mal drew up to full height, wings splayed in terrible arches of darkest pitch. 'Did you read the print of our pact?'

Grant furrowed his brow. 'Uh... yeah.'

'What does it say?'

He thought, quickly, and recited the printed letters of the mail-order kit they'd used. 'You build houses, high towers and strongholds. Throw down the buildings of my enemies, destroy their desires and thoughts and all what they have done, and quickly bring artificers together from all places of the world.'

'What part of that agreement has anything to do with what you're asking me to do?'

'I thought artificers was an old-timey word for tech support?'

'It–' Mal stopped short, overtaken by the kind of groan that Grant heard quite frequently at the local coffee shop, where they never got his order right the first time. 'Yes, it is, but–'

'So what's the problem? Come take a look.'

'The problem, Grant, is that I *bring* artificers. I am not, myself, an artificer. If you want me to call your ISP's service engineer to look at the internet, then I can do that. I am not so skilled as to fix your technical issues myself.'

'Mate, it's the internet,' Grant shrugged. 'It's not rocket science. But fine, whatever. Get us an artificer if it makes you feel better.'

Mal paused. In the dead silence, his beak clicked. 'Really?'

'What?'

'You're seriously asking me to *summon* tech support?'

'Sure, call 'em.' Grant shrugged again. 'Saves me doing it.'

'Are you sure?'

'Didn't I just say that?'

Mal squawked, causing Grant to flinch towards the door. The creature threw his head forward, neck stretching, beak yawning wide, and gruesome caws of laughter punctuating more gobs of the smog.

After the third, Grant was repulsed. After the fourth, he was confused. Then, as the fifth joined the mass, and took on a decidedly human shape, he realised his error. 'Mal, wait – no, this isn't – what are you doing?'

Despite his physical form being clearly unable to speak, Mal's voice sang venomously clear in his mind. 'You asked me to summon an artificer.'

'No, I asked you to call tech support!'

'Is that not what I'm doing?'

'I meant phone them. God! Can you stop that?'

'Nope!' Was that glee Grant heard? 'Not unless you want to scrub half of whomever I've grabbed out of the carpet.'

The last few globs joined the mass on the floor, which now swelled enough to cover the distance between the two of them. It swirled, pulsing excitedly, and from its depths Grant heard an awful screaming. 'Mal, this isn't funny.'

'I think you'll find it is,' Mal rebuked. 'I wonder who we got?'

'You don't know?!'

'I bring artificers,' he said, shrugging. 'Don't much care who they are. Just bring 'em.'

Grant threw his hands up just as Mark opened the door to Mal's room. 'What's the racket?'

'Mal's summoning tech support.'

'What?' Mark said, staring at the roiling substance on the floor. When a most definite hand shape burst from the centre, and began grasping at the carpet, Mark gave a distressed laugh. 'He can do that?'

'Apparently, that's what he's supposed to do.'

'He's supposed to take a look at the internet, not–'

Their argument was cut short by an agonized sort of shrieking that was then muffled by the swirling smog. It began to coalesce and take on a stronger shape and definition. Violent streams of energy crackled across the surface, forming clothes and skin. Finally, with a great sigh of relief from all who bore witness, a man flopped onto the floor. The smog dispersed.

'There,' said Mal, satisfied. 'Tech support.'

The man looked to be in the sort of state whereby he would struggle to remember his own name, let alone deal with technology or support anyone with their ongoing IT issues. 'What did you do to him?' Grant moaned.

'He's fine. Give him a bit to wake up.'

Mark whimpered: 'Is he real?'

Mal snorted, taking a step towards the man on the floor and poking him with a long, taloned toe.

The man groaned, shifted, and threw his arm in Mal's direction. Eyes circled by purple shadow struggled open, and he cleared his throat. 'Whuzzer? Mal?'

'Frank!' Mal crowed. 'Didn't know you were still on shift.'

'I wasn't,' Frank grunted, forcing himself up to his feet. Grant didn't know which was worse: that Mal had summoned an honest to god support engineer into their house, or that the summoning had been for a human being. 'It's the little'un's birthday. Was hoping to go without a call, but… well. You know.'

'Should be an easy one, anyway. These kids–' Mark shouted a protest, but Mal continued as if he wasn't there. '–want their Wi-Fi looked at. D'you mind?'

'They couldn't look at it themselves?'

'Apparently not,' Mal sighed, throwing Grant a malicious glance, with a glint in his beady eye. 'They're insistent we get the best help in the business.'

Frank the support engineer levelled a scowl at the pair. 'Where's your router?'

Mark gestured feebly at the door. Frank trudged past. When the door slammed behind them, Grant rounded on Mal. 'Why did you do that?'

'You asked me to,' Mal replied, with an indignant flap of his wings. 'You wanted support, I brought you an artificer to support you.'

'I asked you to *call*–'

'You're gonna learn your lesson if I make the phone call for you, are you?' Mal cackled. 'At least the lordling had the courage to understand his failings.'

'Lordling?' Mark asked.

Grant waved his hand. 'Go check on Frank.'

Mark shrugged, leaving. Grant pinched the bridge of his nose. 'It's the internet. We didn't need a support engineer out here.'

'Doesn't matter what you need,' Mal replied. 'You asked me to call support, so I called support.'

'Can we send him back?'

Mal's cackling rose again, punctuated by the clack of his beak. 'What?' asked Grant. 'What?'

'The look on your face–'

'*Mal.* Tell me we can send him back.'

'Oh sure, sure,' Mal rasped, catching his breath. 'You'll need to pay for his flights, like, but you can send him back whenever.'

'His flights?'

'Yes – come on, Grant, I'm not in the habit of repeating myself.'

'We can't just...'

'Didn't you read–'

'Read the text of the pact?' Grant groaned. 'Right. Yes. God...'

'Is not much help to you here, mate.'

***

Grant left Mal's room, chased by the creature's incessant cackling. It pecked at his ears as he tried to steady his breathing and figure out the full iimplications of what Mal's rascality – and his arrogance – had visited upon them.

He found Mark and Frank in the hall, Frank examining

their disconnected router. 'Nothing's damaged,' he concluded. 'What did you say the problem was?'

'Internet's out,' said Mark, shooting Grant an exasperated look behind Frank's back. 'I don't know, mate, it just went.'

'Did you check the service status page of your provider?' Frank asked, the syllables structured in such an orderly, recited way that they supressed the otherwise clear frustration he showed at his current circumstances.

'I… no, I didn't check. Grant, did you?'

'Don't pin this on me,' Grant snapped, folding his arms. 'You asked me to speak to Mal. This is on you.'

Mark huffed, hunching over his phone to check. As the seconds passed, the sound of Mark's mobile keyboard the only thing filling the air, Grant did his best to avoid Frank's eye. Part of him knew, instinctively, what Mark was going to find. 'So, uh,' he began, clearing his throat, 'where are you from?'

'My family's in Norway,' Frank deadpanned.

Grant blanched. '*Norway!?*'

'Oh, aye. My father and his father before him,' he nodded. 'But I live in Stockport.'

Grant's middling achievements in geography filled his sigh with relief. 'That's not too far from here.'

'What's our password?' Mark blurted, out of nowhere.

'It's your account!' Grant returned.

'Oh, right. Hang on…'

Mark turned his back on the pair and stalked off, muttering something about resetting his password. 'He's not very good at this, is he?' Frank muttered.

'He tries.' Grant shook his head. 'So you know Mal?'

'Oh, aye. Engineers get to know their locals pretty well, given their habit of ripping us through space and time for urgent support items. How bored is he?'

'Less bored than he was, I'm sure.'

'Word of advice,' Frank offered, 'just roll with it.'

'You're kidding – after what he's done to you? You want me

to just let it slide?'

Frank chortled, 'It's not the worst time he's grabbed me. Once I was in bed with this lad, and–'

'He didn't!'

'He *did*,' Frank laughed. 'Never done my belt up so quickly.'

'I'm amazed you still work with him.'

'Don't have a choice. Mal doesn't care which artificer he brings, just so long as he brings one, right?'

'So he's said.'

'Right. You read your pact, didn't you?'

Grant sighed, feeling a knot of tension in the middle of his forehead. 'Yep.'

'So you know this is just part of the pact?'

'Huh?'

Frank smiled, kindly. 'When you've got a mo, go read the pact. Properly. It'll make your life a lot less stressful.'

'Got it!' yelled Mark, turning triumphantly back to the rest of the room. 'Says here that there's a service outage for planned maintenance. Oh, wait. That's…'

'Mark…' Grant growled.

'That's me done, then,' Frank declared, reaching out to clap Grant on the shoulder. 'Nothing to be done except wait for the maintenance to end.'

'How are you going to get home?'

'Oh, don't worry about that,' he said. 'Couple a few doors down has Bathim summoned. I'll call in a favour.'

'That easy?'

'Perks of knowing the locals,' Frank winked. 'You could learn a thing or two.'

***

Frank went back downstairs, Grant and Mark following behind in quiet argument. Mal's cackling still echoed from his room, a grating noise that lorded his victory over the pair, and exacerbated their squabbling. 'Alright, then,' said Frank, much louder than any voice in the house, 'I'll be off. If your problem persists after the maintenance ends…'

'We'll call the support line,' Grant finished.

'Atta boy. You kids behave yourselves, now – and don't pay Mal any mind. Let him wear himself out and you'll be back to normal.'

'I heard that!' Mal's breathless voice wheezed under the laughter, scraping once more against Grant's mind.

Grant winced, and rubbed at his temple. 'Thanks again,' he said, holding the door open for Frank. When the door had closed, Mal's laughter finally began to peter out.

'What now?' Mark mumbled.

'I don't care.' Grant shook his head. 'Go watch a movie or something.'

Mark shuffled off, while Grant went back to the lounge, where he dug into the cabinet under the television. He scattered crumpled bills and full folders until, at last, he found the weathered parchment that had arrived with the summoning pack.

'*Malphas*,' Grant read, '*the Thirty-Ninth Spirit… He can build Houses… bring to thy Knowledge Enemies' Desires and Thoughts… giveth Good Familiars.*'

He traced his finger over the penultimate line. '*If thou makest a Sacrifice unto him he will receive it kindly and willingly, but he will deceive him that*– oh, you've got to be kidding.'

Grant stormed back to Mal's room, parchment in hand, and barged in. Mal was reclined against his usual corner, tablet back in hand, movie watching. 'Oi!'

Mal jumped, giving a startled squawk. 'What now?'

'*If thou makest a Sacrifice unto him he will receive it kindly and willingly, but he will deceive him that doth it,*' Grant recited accusingly.

'Yes?'

'You lied to us? Tricking me into summoning Frank, making me think we were stuck with booking his flight home – that's all part of the game to you?'

'Only sometimes,' Mal said casually. 'You found out what was wrong with your internet, didn't you?'

'You ripped a guy from his home!'

'It's Frank! Did he look like he cared?' Mal cackled. 'Call it my service charge if it helps you sleep better. You signed up for it when you summoned me.'

'No we didn't!'

'Grant', Mal's voice seethed, worsening the discomfort it caused, 'I hate repeating myself almost as much as I enjoyed Frank's face when he woke up here, so I'll ask this one more time. Did you read the pact?'

'That's why we're having this conversation!' Grant shouted indignantly.

'No, we're having this conversation because you *haven't* read the pact. Not properly.'

'What?'

A jet of sulphurous smog spewed from Mal's mouth as he sighed. 'What part of pact don't you understand? Should I crack open a dictionary for you? Here, let me search for it on the internet I helped you fix.'

'I know what a pact is!'

'Then why are you complaining? You signed up to every word of the pact when you summoned me.'

'Why is 'The demon you summon will lie to you' part of that?'

'Because you mortals are astonishingly easy to trick,' he cackled. 'You won't believe some of the things we got you to agree to back when. Crocell, for all his powers, got his pact by agreeing to heat up water and discovering baths. Can you imagine what his job's like now?'

'Can't we change the pact? Make it more modern and sensible?' Grant suggested, the very thought of his request feeling feeble.

'And miss out on your dumb face when you realise what I'm doing?' Mal shook his head, black feathers rustling. 'I think not. Besides, you already signed up. What could I possibly gain by changing the terms now?'

'Is this how it's gonna be every time? You sneaking as much stress as you can into every request we make?'

'If it's any comfort, you're at your funniest when you fall for it,' Mal joked. 'Do you need another artificer?'

'No! Absolutely not, you're not summoning anyone else.'

'Not now, at least.'

'Not ever! We'll take care of ourselves.'

'Mmhm.' Mal sounded unconvinced. He returned to his tablet and tapped it with his beak, causing his video to start again. 'You'd be breaking my circle if that were true.'

'I–' Grant stopped short of his next words. 'You're the worst.'

Mal made a mocking coo of his insult, pretending to shudder. Incensed, Grant marched from the room and slammed the door as loudly as he could. He took one breath. Two. Three. He tried counting to ten, but absolutely nothing seemed to bring him down from his fury.

Maybe Frank was right, he mused. All he could do was let it go.

***

'Grant?'

'WHAT?' The voice that shrieked from the very bottom of his lungs barely seemed like his own. 'WHAT COULD YOU *POSSIBLY* WANT NOW?'

Mark stuck his head out from the kitchen door. 'Jesus, man. Was just gonna say the microwave's busted.'

'Great. Fantastic. Just what I wanted to hear.'

Mark stared at Grant, bewildered. 'Everything alright?'

Grant opened his mouth to respond, but a corner of

crumpled parchment clutched in his fist gave him pause. He considered the exact wording of the last line and, like a wave, revelation washed over him. He found a smile. 'I'm fine. It's your turn, right?'

'Uh... sure.'

'Alright. Great.' Grant's smile widened. 'Go talk to Mal about it.'

About the Authors

Nadine Dalton-West

Nadine Dalton-West is the author of BFS award-shortlisted 'The Women's Song' (in the *Fight Like a Girl* collection), 'Rusalka' (in *The Book of Orm*) and 'The House in Brooklyn' (in *The Book of Witches*) all published by Kristell Ink. She is learning to play the cello, and is happiest near animals or large bodies of water. She is on Twitter and Instagram as @andiekarenina, and her website is https://nadinedaltonwest.com.

Gabriel Wisdom

Gabriel Wisdom is a financier, pilot, former radio disc jockey, and a fiction writer, www.GabrielWisdom.com. Gabriel's earliest recollection of demonic behavior occurred while he was introducing the headliner at a rock concert. Ten thousand fans gasped when the band's lead singer tossed him off the stage. His rock DJ persona as Alice Wisdom was portrayed in Cameron Crowe's Oscar winning screenplay, *Almost Famous*, from DreamWorks / Sony Pictures. Gabe's writing credits include *Wisdom on Value Investing*, published by John Wiley & Sons. He is a PhD in Creative Writing candidate under the supervision of Dr A.J. Dalton at Middlesex University, London.

Elyn Joy

Elyn Joy is an American author from Denver, Colorado. Her published works include two children's books, *Everyone Has a Point of View* (2018) and *Once Upon a Pigeon and Other Retold Fables* (C.R. Success Learning/Barnes & Noble, 2017), two health education books, *The Gluten-Free Parent's Survival Guide* (2019) and *The Gluten-Free Teen's Survival Guide* (2021), as well as several articles for health/lifestyle magazines in the U.S. and Canada. Whatever the project, Elyn tends to fight for—and write for—the misunderstood 'other' (be it human, animal, or even demon!). Visit her at www.elynjoy.com, Elyn Joy (Facebook), or @elynjoy (Insta).

A J Dalton

A J Dalton (the 'A' is for Adam) is a prize-winning author of science fiction and fantasy. He has published twelve books to date, including *The Book of Orm*, *The Book of Angels*, *The Book of Dragons* and *The Book of Witches* with Kristell Ink, the *Empire of the Saviours* trilogy with Gollancz, *I am a Small God* with Admanga Publishing, and *The Satanic in Science Fiction and Fantasy* with Luna Press Publishing. His website is www.ajdalton.eu, where there is much to entertain fans of SFF. He is to be found hanging out with his cat Cleopatra in London, init.

J.McDonald

'Upon Reflection' is J.McDonald's debut piece. Having spent an inordinate amount of time and money on reading the works of others, this new Canadian author decided it was time to try to give back to a community that has provided countless hours of enjoyment. McDonald has a Bachelor of Arts Honours degree in English, a Bachelor of Education degree, and recently completed a Master's in Novel Writing. When not chained to a computer, video games and movies are usually the order of the day. For more pieces like this, check out JMcDonaldWorks.com or follow j.mcdonaldworks on Instagram.

Michael Conroy

Michael Conroy is a British writer fleeing debt and scandal, on the continent. His current work in progress is a novel about Italy, China, and SARS. Visit his website www.siriuseditorial.com for information on editing and copywriting services.

Isabella Hunter

Isabella Hunter loves all things occult, macabre, and demonic, and those themes are common to all her stories. First publishing 'The Dragon Daughter' in *The Book of Dragons* back in 2017, she has gone on to write for several different publishers during the past few years. Her horror story 'Husk' found itself included in the *Creep* anthology by CultureCult and the 2019 reading list of the Horror Writers' Association. She also contributed 'At the Witching Hour' to *The Book of Witches* in 2020. She spends most days agonising over the different stories she wants to write and working in a call centre. She runs a small blog, where she shares experiences from her everyday life: isabellahunter.blog. She can also be found on facebook under Isabella Hunter and on twitter under @EvanovaLev.

Matt Beeson

Matt Beeson is father to Brandon, husband to Nola; these are the things he knows for certain. He is a professional risk consultant, primarily occupied with preventing things from burning down and blowing up. This is in stark contrast to his efforts in writing fiction, wherein he rather enjoys things burning down and blowing up. *The Book of Demons* is his second leap into the now-slightly-less-unknown world of fiction writing; he's really rather starting to enjoy it and very much hopes you do too. His previous work (not including technical reports and papers) can be found in *The Book of Witches*: 'Three Conversations or How I Burned your Mother'. In his spare time he likes to read lots of things – his tastes are eclectic – while sitting, preferably. Sometimes just sitting will do. He was once a musician and hopes to be one again someday. Until then there is always chocolate and coffee. He is occasionally to be found on Twitter (@Phaeduck).

JES Simpson

JES Simpson, also known as John, lives in North London and daydreams about houseboats. This is his first publication: although he has always been a world builder, he only recently started writing those worlds down. His first novel, *A Fire in the Night*, is coming along nicely, thank you for asking. You can tweet him @Geeksimpson. He'd like that.

Nozomi Okumura

Nozomi Okumura (@NozomiOkumura) adores fantasy of every shape and style, and they long to write stories in that vein for as long as humanly possible. They crawled from the depths of their Twitter feed long enough to string some words together, and 'Solomon's Prime Key' is the result – a result they are extremely excited to share with you!

Acknowledgements

A whole slew of people have helped put together the *The Book of Demons*. I'd like to thank...

- Sammy HK Smith of Kristell Ink, whose tolerance and good faith are equally rare amongst publishers
- Charlotte Pang, who produced the great book cover
- Matt Beeson, Michael Conroy, Isabella Hunter, Gabriel Wisdom, Nadine Dalton-West, J.McDonald, Matt Beeson, JES Simpson, Elyn Joy and Nozomi Okumura, my inspiring co-authors, who have contributed their work, hearts and minds in return for a small pile of groats
- Mum and Dad, who continue to support the literary ambitions of their son against all good reason and common sense
- Nadine Dalton-West, my beautiful wife, whose only flaw is that she writes better than me
- all those fantasy fans who keep insisting it's all worth it
- and, as per the dedication, every woman, person or animal who has suffered persecution or demonization for who they are!

I humbly salute you all!

A J Dalton

Also by A.J. Dalton

from Kristell Ink Publishing

The Book of Orm

This exciting new collection brings together the writing talents of international fantasy author A J Dalton, Nadine West (Bridport Anthology) and Matt White (prize-winning scriptwriter). Magic, myth and heroic mayhem combine in a world that is eerily familiar yet beautifully liberating.

The Book of Witches

Have you ever been persecuted, demonized, drowned or burnt at the stake? Witches have, and here are their stories.

This exciting new collection brings together the writing talents of international fantasy author A J Dalton, Adam Lively (prize-winning novelist), Nadine Dalton-West (friend to gods and demons), Garry Coulthard (enemy of mediocrity), Isabella Hunter (champion of the unchampioned), Michael Conroy (scion of the Ninth House) and Matt Beeson (right hand of the Guardian of Azeroth) and Michael Victor Bowman (widely worshipped by those who know about such things).

The Book of Angels

Would you want to be an angel? The pay's terrible and you get nothing but complaints from dissatisfied mortals. This exciting new collection brings together the writing talents of international fantasy author A J Dalton, Matt White (prize-winning scriptwriter), Caimh McDonnell (writer for Mock the Week), Sammy HK Smith (friend to gods and demons), Andrew Coulthard (award-nominated short story writer) and Michael Bowman (widely worshipped by those who know about such things).

The Book of Dragons

He saw dragons everywhere, and that was why they'd put him in a secure unit. They told him there was no such thing as dragons. But he'd seen unprovoked attacks on the street, violence break out in an apparently quiet bar, rage overtake people on crowded pavements, and supposed peace-keepers use shocking degrees of force. In such moments, the beasts revealed themselves. They could be glimpsed louring from beneath ridged brows, snarling in the corner of your eye and leering between your rapid and confused blinks. You had to be quick, mind, and know what to look for. But once you knew about them, it was somehow harder for them to convince you that you'd imagined what you'd seen, that you'd been mistaken, or that it had all been some trick of the light. Once you knew about them and properly believed in them, it seemed they had less power over you, less ability to blind you to them and less general impossibility. What really worried him, though, was whether they suspected he saw them. And if they began to suspect, what might they then do to him?

kristell-ink.com

Printed in Great Britain
by Amazon

65316270R00119